ONLY IF YOU LET ME

MONICA WALTERS

Edited by
PROSPER PUB & DESIGN

B. LOVE PUBLICATIONS

Edited by: Prosper Pub & Design

B. LOVE PUBLICATIONS

Visit bit.ly/readBLP to join our mailing list!

B. Love Publications - where Authors celebrate black men, black women, and black love.

To submit a manuscript for consideration, email your first three chapters to blovepublications@gmail.com with SUBMISSION as the subject.

Let's connect on social media!

Facebook - B. Love Publications

Twitter - @blovepub

Instagram - @blovepublications

INTRODUCTION

Hello Readers!

I'm so happy you've chosen to read this body of work. It is a spin-off from a previous novel titled, Say He's the One. While it's not necessary to read Say He's the One before reading this one, it will help you better understand some situations in this story.

It also has graphic sex scenes that are sure to leave you feeling some type of way. If sexual lewdness offends you, please don't continue to read.

That being said, I hope you enjoy it!

Monica

PROLOGUE

nsley

"I'M SORRY, Ansley, but she's pregnant."

The plate I held in my hand with Jonathan's dinner on it, slipped from my fingers and crashed to the floor. Two months ago, I'd found out he was cheating on me. Now for him to sit here in my face and say his hoe was pregnant was some hurtful shit.

He'd gotten home late as usual. When I'd called to find out what was taking him so long to get home, he said he had a meeting that ran late. Being a supervisor for the City of Beaumont's drainage district, that was a common occurrence. It turned out, that meeting was with his hoe, Ranika.

"Ansley, I plan to continue to take care of my family. I want us to remain together."

My eyes went dark like a damned shark when they went into attack mode. I glanced around the kitchen and living room to make sure neither of our three children were close enough to hear what I had to say. "You must be a stupid mutha-fucka if you think I'm going to hang around to watch you raise a baby with someone else."

"Ansley... please. You forgave me for the infidelity. I haven't slept with her since. I didn't know she would get pregnant."

"Yes, I forgave you, but this changes everything. That bitch is going to forever be in our lives. I won't be able to handle that."

I watched him drag his hands down his face while breathing deeply. Just because I forgave him, didn't mean that all was well. Jonathan had been the love of my life since I was in the ninth grade. I'd never cheated on him, and as far as I knew, he'd never cheated on me. We'd been married for the past seven years, and I thought we were both happy.

The emotions that took over my body when I followed him from work to her house were unfamiliar. The kids were with my mother because I told her I had errands to run. Seeing that whore open the door and kiss his lips before he could get inside, killed my soul. I gave him about five minutes, just until I could really get worked up, then I got out my car and banged on her door.

I never thought in a million years that would be me. When she opened it, and I asked, *Where's Jonathan,* the bitch had the nerve to cop a whole attitude. Before I knew it, I'd punched her in her got damned throat, then chin checked his ass. I walked out that house like a boss, but the minute I drove away, the hurt set in.

Jonathan didn't know what it was like to feel like you weren't good enough. My self-esteem took a huge hit after that. I didn't feel desirable or beautiful. One thing I could give him, the hoe was cute and curvy. Usually, men downgraded when it came to looks. That only made me feel worse about my abdominal pudge, stretch marks, and scars from my C-section. I thought I was doing everything a wife was supposed to do. When he'd gotten home, he'd cried and apologized, begging me not to leave him. I didn't give him an answer that day, but eventually, I succumbed to the thought that no one else wanted me and I might as well stay.

"Ansley, please. I don't want to lose you. I know my actions from two months ago don't say that, but I promise to continue to show you how much you mean to me. I love you."

"Mooooommyyyyy," our two-year-old daughter, Alana, sang out.

"I'm coming, baby."

I cut my eyes at Jonathan, then attempted to walk past him. He could clean all that shit up from the floor. I was done catering to him. As I walked past, he attempted to grab my hand. Jerking away from him, I continued walking to my baby. When I got to her room, she was all wrapped up in her sheets and blanket. I'd just made that bed.

"Alana? Where are you?"

She was quiet. She often played hide and seek with me. My five-year-old twin boys were always independent. They played with each other and never really craved my attention like she did. Finally, I sat on the floor next to where I knew she was. "I don't know what I'm going to do if I can't find my baby," I whined sarcastically.

"Boo!" she yelled as she threw the covers off her head.

I laughed, then brought her to my lap. She put her hand to my face. "Mommy wook sad."

I hated that she could always tell how I was feeling. Standing to my feet, I asked, "You wanna go to the park?"

"Yay! What about Sage and Gawett?"

She never wanted to leave the twins out. Sage and Garrett. Alana still had a hard time with ls and rs. "Go and ask them if they wanna come."

She ran out of her room as I followed, meeting Jonathan in the hallway. The puppy dog eyes were only making me angrier. I walked past him as the kids came in the hall. "Are you guys ready?"

"Yay!" they all yelled.

I walked to the kitchen as they told their dad bye and grabbed my keys and purse. I guess this would be my Christmas gift. It was only a couple of months away. After Jonathan helped strap Alana in her car seat, the boys got in their booster seats and buckled up. "Ansley, can we please talk, seriously, when you get back?"

Instead of answering him, I closed my door, then backed out of the driveway.

After getting to the complex on College Street, the kids nearly lost their minds when they saw the park. I laughed and helped them out. As they took off for the slides, I could feel someone watching me. When I turned, I saw a young guy heading toward me. I wasn't in the mood for any foolishness. My phone was in my hand, waiting to dial 9-1-1 or my younger brother, Remo. "I'm sorry. I didn't mean to startle you. You just looked so beautiful, I had to approach."

I eased up a little, then smiled slightly as I glanced at the kids playing. "What's your name?"

"Ansley. Yours?"

"Jayden."

"Nice to meet you, Jayden, but I have three kids to tend to. Plus, you look way younger than me."

"Looks can be deceiving. I just turned twenty-four."

"I'm almost thirty."

"Damn. You look good, Ansley. Can I have your number?"

I looked over at the kids again. What did I have to lose by giving him my number? At least someone was showing me attention. Jayden made me feel extremely sexy the way he looked me over. Slowly, he slid my phone from my hands and dialed his number. I heard it ring, but my eyes never left his. He was so charming.

"Ansley, can I call you later?"

"Yeah," I responded, barely above a whisper.

He grabbed my hand and stared at me while licking his lips. "I can't wait to get to know you. How old are your kids?"

"The boys are five, and my daughter is two. I should get to them before they notice I'm not over there."

"Okay. I'll be over here playing ball and admiring you from a distance."

I could feel my face heat up as he ran his fingers down my arm. It had been a long time since I'd even thought of entertaining anyone other than Jonathan, but being noticed by someone else made me feel amazing. I smiled, then walked over to my kids as they played.

After playing at the park, we ate at Chick-Fil-A. When we got home, Jonathan wasn't there. Figures. I had yet to let a tear fall. Truth was, although I'd forgiven him for his infidelity, I wasn't over it. Trust was now a foreign word in my vocabulary. I ran the boys some bath water in the hallway bathroom and brought Alana to my room. As she played in the tub, my mind traveled to one of the most devastating times of my life.

I'd walked in on my dad and his whore. Seven years ago, I'd just gotten back from my honeymoon two weeks before, and my mama was on a trip. If he could cheat on my mother, who was perfect in me and Remo's book, who was I? I wasn't the woman my mama was by a long shot, but if Daddy could cheat on her, then Jonathan had probably *been* cheating on me.

Listening to Albert Pierre apologize to me that day did nothing for me as a woman. I couldn't tell my mama what I'd seen, because I knew it would only hurt her. She would never leave my daddy. So, that day after watching my daddy beg me not to tell mama, and cry and promise me that it wouldn't happen again, I agreed to keep it to myself. I did tell him that if it ever happened again and I found out about it, I would let Mama know that it wasn't the first time.

So, when I noticed that Jonathan was wearing cologne to work more often than usual, and money was missing from the account that he couldn't account for, I knew some foul shit was going on. He rarely wanted to go places as a family anymore, and he was always on his phone. Before following him that day, I already knew.

After washing Alana up and getting her ready for bed, I texted Jonathan to see where he was. *Where are you?*

He responded, *I had to go run an errand.*

His ass must have thought I was some dumb hoe. He was out with that bitch. I didn't respond to him. My phone started ringing, and I thought it was him calling me. When I looked at the caller ID, I realized it was Jayden. My palms got sweaty, and my heart rate increased as I answered. "Hello?"

"Hello. Ansley?"

"Yes."

"It's Jayden. How's your evening going?"

"It's going okay. I just got my daughter ready for bed."

"Oh. You need to call me back?"

"If you don't mind. I need to check on the boys."

"Okay. I'll be waiting, Ansley."

I loved the way he said my name. It almost sounded like he was whining the way he drug out the first syllable. Ending the call, I checked on the boys, and they were putting on their PJ's. I helped them in bed, then kissed their heads. After going back to Alana's room to kiss her goodnight, I headed back to my bedroom. She was already conked out. They'd played so hard at the park, they were all tired.

After taking my shower, I laid in bed, staring at my phone. Two wrongs didn't make a right. I wasn't fucking nobody though. *Besides, It's just a phone call, Ans.* I knew Jayden was interested in me though, and I didn't bother to tell him I was married. Honestly, I didn't know how long I would be. Going against the voice of reason, I called him. "Hey, Ansley."

My face heated up. "Hi."

"The kids all settled?"

"Yes."

"Good. I'm glad you called back."

"Are you? What could you possibly want with a woman almost six years older than you with three children?"

"Well, regardless of the facts you stated, I think you're a beautiful woman. I was curious to know if you're as beautiful on the inside as you are on the outside."

"Don't try to run game on me, Jayden. I'm too old for that shit."

"I'm not trying to run game. I'm just stating the facts. Your age doesn't bother me. It's not like you're fifty. I love kids, and they love me, so that doesn't bother me either."

I was silent for a moment, so he asked, "You still there? I scared you off?"

"I'm here, Jayden. You seem like a nice guy."

"I am."

"Do you have any kids?"

"Nope. Are your kids' fathers in their life?"

"Their father is involved," I said, placing emphasis on father.

"My bad. I didn't mean anything by that."

"I guess I'll let you make it. I have to get up pretty early tomorrow, Jayden. Can we talk another day?"

"Sure. I'm off tomorrow, so I'll hit you up. Get some rest, beautiful."

"Thank you. Talk to you soon."

The way my body reacted to him, it felt like I was about to start dating someone for the first time. I thought back to his chocolate skin and gorgeous smile and how he licked his thick lips. Jayden had boyish good looks that he topped off with a perfect mustache and goatee. The dimple in his left cheek made his smile that much more amazing. It didn't take much for him to tower over me, but he had to be around six feet, give or take an inch.

I plugged my phone to the charger, then yawned and sunk underneath my comforter. Before I could doze off, I heard the back door open and close. Jonathan was back. Hopefully, he didn't try to sleep in here with me. I laid in bed with my eyes shut as the door opened and closed.

Although my eyes were closed, I could feel him in front of me. His hand glided across my cheek. He whispered, "I wish none of this ever happened. You mean everything to me, Ans. I'm so sorry."

His words caused something to stir deep within me. *Was he really sorry?* My eyes opened slowly to find him on his knees in front of me. He swiped the stray curl from my face. "I love you, Ans."

I swallowed the lump in my throat, refusing to let a tear fall. I'd cried so much when I first found out he was cheating on me. I was all cried out. He kissed my forehead. Looking into his eyes, I saw the Jonathan Malveaux I'd first fallen in love with at West Brook High School in the ninth grade. There was so much remorse in them, it pulled at my soul.

Lifting my hand and resting it on his cheek, I stroked it with my thumb. "Will you please let me start over? I know I can never make up for what I did, but I wanna at least try."

"Let's just take one day at a time. Okay?"

He nodded, then kissed my head again. Standing to his feet, he walked away to the bathroom. I listened to the shower start, then thought, *Where in the hell had he gone?* Unconditional love had invaded my being and was gonna render me ignorant as hell. Those words were beautiful, but not beautiful enough. Actions spoke louder than words.

When he came out the restroom, I went in immediately. "Where were you, Jon?"

"When?"

I rolled my eyes at his stalling attempt. "When me and the kids got here, you were gone. Where were you?"

"I'd just gone to get gas and think about how I would proceed in my life. Ranika will need my help raising the kid I had a part in creating. Trying to figure out how I will handle that and keep you happy at the same time, is making me plan my next steps carefully. I don't want to lose you, Ans, regardless of what my past actions have spoken."

Okay, maybe I could let unconditional love invade my mind and heart for now. I nodded, then closed my eyes. When he got in the bed, he slid his arm over my side, spooning me. Feelings of hurt and despair soon dissipated and turned into ones of love, forgiveness, and healing.

———

THE NEXT DAY was going by rather quickly. I worked in a doctor's office, billing insurances for patient expenses. Today had been busier than normal, and I was ready to get some much-needed rest. Last night only yielded about three full hours of sleep for me. After taking Sage and Garrett to school and Alana to daycare, I headed straight to work. Jonathan was leaving when I got the kids up. He said for me not to worry about dinner, that he would take care of everything this evening.

I supposed he was gonna be leaving work early. As I sat in the lounge eating lunch, my phone alerted me of a text message. I opened it to see, *Hi Ansley. I hope your day is going well* from Jayden. I should've told him I was married. He was so cute though and such a sweetheart. Instead of messaging him back, I called. "Hello?"

"Hi, Jayden. Are you busy?"

"Not at all. How are you?"

"I'm great. What about you?"

"I'm good. I'm glad you called."

"Really? Why?"

"Your voice is so soothing and sexy."

I felt the heat rush to my face. *God, he was the sexy one.* Bringing him into my shit was a bad decision, but there was no way I was letting him go now. I had to get to know him. "Thank you, Jayden."

"Damn, girl."

"What?"

"Don't be saying my name like that either."

I giggled. "Like what?"

"You know what'chu doin' to me," he said with a slight chuckle. "Where do you work?"

"I work at a doctor's office, handling insurance claims."

"That's cool. You like it?"

"It has its days, but for the most part, I like it. Where do you work that affords you off days in the middle of the week?"

"I work at ExxonMobil as a process operator."

Shit. I hope he didn't know my brother. Remo had been working there for five years or so. Instead of asking him if he knew Remo, I asked, "When do you go back to work?"

"Tomorrow. Can I see you today?"

"Umm... After I get my kids from school and daycare, it's non-stop until they go to bed at eight-thirty."

"I understand. Maybe I can see you this weekend."

"Maybe so."

"I like you, Ansley."

"I like you too. What do you do for fun?"

"Not too much. I play basketball and kick it with friends mostly. What about you?"

"I'm mostly with my kids or my brother. Everything seems to revolve around the little ones. Do you have any siblings?"

"Not biologically. I have a step-brother and a step-sister."

"Oh okay. Well, as much as I hate to, I have to go back to work."

"Oh, you hate to?"

"Yeah. I was enjoying our conversation."

"Me too. If you have time, call me later."

"I'll call you when I get off."

"Okay, Ansley. I'll be waiting."

My face heated up again. "Okay. Bye."

I smiled as I headed back to my desk. Seeing roses sitting there made me feel guilty though. I was sure Jonathan had them delivered. As I pulled the card from the stem, my hand trembled. "Those are so beautiful," my nosy-ass co-worker said. "He must be in the doghouse."

"Mind yo' business."

They knew I didn't discuss my personal shit at work, but this heifer was always trying to push the envelope. I didn't bite my tongue with her either. Finding a way to tell her off without adding my usual curse words was challenging at times, though. Opening the card and reading what it said, was causing my emotions to come to the fore-front. *I love you, Ansley. I plan to spend the rest of my life showing you how much I mean that. Love, Jonathan.*

Taking a deep breath, I sat at my desk and resumed paperwork, hoping the second half of the day went by as fast as the first half did. My phone vibrated. *I can't wait to hear your voice again.* I smiled at Jayden's message, then resumed my day.

———

JAYDEN and I had talked off and on for a month now, and for the past three days in a row. I hadn't been able to give him as much time as I would have liked to, though. The kids had their Christmas sing-along today, so I'd taken off work. Just as I was about to text Jayden, he texted me. My worst fear had been confirmed. *I can't talk to you no more. Why didn't you tell me you were married?*

Taking a deep breath, I responded immediately. *It's complicated, Jayden.*

Damn it, Ansley. I'm feeling you. Remo will kill me. Oh, by the way, your brother is one of my best friends. Smh.

Although they were only words in a text message, I could feel the hurt in them. Jonathan had been the perfect husband the past month, but my heart was feeling numb toward him. At first, I thought it was because of my interest in Jayden, but after reanalyzing my situation, I knew it was because I was still hurt. My heart was choosing to protect itself from being hurt again. My phone began ringing, and I knew it was Remo. I looked at the caller ID to confirm my suspicion.

Remo was my younger brother by five years, but he often treated me like I was his little sister. He looked up to me in a lot of ways though. Having a loving family was something he wanted, and it was one thing he always complimented me on. I'd never told him or my parents about Jonathan cheating on me. I texted Jayden again. *I'm sorry. Please don't stop talking to me.*

Starting my car, I headed to the school to the Christmas program feeling horrible for not telling Jayden about Jonathan. So horrible in fact, I didn't hear a song they sang. "Mommy, okay?"

I looked down at Alana and forced a smile. "Mommy's fine, baby."

Lightly bouncing her on my lap to the beat of the music took my mind off things for a moment. Sage and Garrett were stealing the show with their moves and loud singing. My children gave me so much joy. The boys were identical and looked just like Jonathan. Alana looked like her daddy too, in my opinion, although people swore she was the spitting image of me. She only had my complexion and hair.

As I got some footage with my phone, Alana decided she would participate in "Jingle Bells." It was too cute, and everyone around us thought so too. Once the program was over, we headed to the boys' classroom for their party. I did my best to socialize and stay involved with the festivities, but I couldn't help but think about Jayden.

I tried texting him again. *I'm sorry, Jayden. Please talk to me.* Maybe he'd blocked me. Well, that was that. My mind was confused as to whether I would stay with Jonathan because my heart just wasn't in it anymore. I loved him, but I didn't want to be in love with him anymore. My spirit was crushed, and it didn't seem I was able to repair it as long as I was in a relationship with Jonathan.

Jayden was young, but I felt a great connection to him. Being six years older than him didn't seem to matter at all. It wasn't evident in our conversation topics, either.

After getting the kids situated at home; fed, cleaned, and put to bed, I called my brother. "Hello?"

"Hey, Me-Mo. What's up?"

I tried to sound unbothered like I didn't know why he wanted me to call. I'd been calling him Me-Mo since he was two years old, mispronouncing his own name. "Don't hey Me-Mo me. What the hell going on wit'chu, Ansley?"

"What are you talking about?"

"Jayden. Now tell me."

I remained quiet. My mouth had gone dry, and I honestly didn't know what to say without telling him about Jonathan. "So, you gon' just throw your whole marriage away for some dick?"

Damn, he was angry with me. He'd never spoken to me so harshly, and it caused the tears to spring from my eyes. "Remo, stop. You don't know what I go through in this house."

"So why don't you tell me, so I can stop assuming shit!"

"Jonathan got a woman pregnant," I said softly.

Now, it was his turn to be speechless. He took an unsteady breath. "Damn, Ans. Why didn't you tell me?"

"I'm embarrassed. I never thought this would be my life. Jonathan's not perfect, but cheating was never something I expected. Not only did he cheat, but that shit will be thrown in my face as soon as the baby is born. So, yes. I met Jayden at the rec. It felt good to be noticed, especially by someone younger than me. My self-esteem had plummeted. I'm not enough for Jonathan, and that shit is devastating to me."

"I'm sorry, sis. I really am. But foolin' around with Jayden isn't the answer. Why haven't you left him?"

"I'm scared. I've never lived on my own, and now I have three small children to take care of. Remo, financially I can't make it without him."

"Yes, you can. First, you can start by filing child support on his ass. You ought to be able to get at least a grand a month. You know I'll help you. Plus, you work. You know Mama and Daddy will help you too."

"I just feel like a failure, Me-Mo," I said through my tears.

"Don't do that, sis."

"I have to go, Remo. Alana is in there screaming at the boys."

"Okay. I'm gonna call you tomorrow, okay?"

"Okay."

Talking to someone about what was going on was therapeutic for me. I didn't really have friends, because I was always so busy trying to take care of my family. Crying was a whole 'notha issue. Remo was the only person I really felt comfortable crying in front of, but it was still rare that I did. Going to the boys' room, I found Alana in there picking with them, putting her finger in their faces. "Alana, why are you in here?"

"Gawett mean!"

"Come on here, girl," I said, pulling her out of their room.

After getting her situated in her room, I heard Jonathan come in. Working things out with him would be ideal for my kids, but I didn't know if that was something I wanted. Could I be happy with him after this? I didn't think so. I would always wonder if he was still screwing that bitch. If I were just a little more ratchet, I'd go to her house and beat her pregnant ass.

———

WORK WAS SLOW TODAY. It was almost Christmas, and I just wanted to be done so I could enjoy time off. The past two weeks had been hard as hell. Living with Jonathan had been a lot harder than I thought it would be. Even though he seemed to be trying, it wasn't enough. For the sake of my kids' mental health and mine, it was probably best that we threw in the towel on what was left of our marriage.

Remo wasn't happy with me for staying as long as I had, but he didn't get it. He didn't understand how big of a decision this was for me. If it were just me, I would have left the moment I found out he was cheating. I had kids to think about. I'd sacrifice my happiness for theirs every time. Besides, if my dad could cheat on my mama, I was convinced that all men cheated. I was becoming bitter, and my kids didn't deserve that version of me.

As I processed a couple of insurance payments, I heard a familiar voice and laugh. *What the fuck?* I know his ass didn't bring that bitch to my job. Standing from my desk and walking to the front, I saw Jonathan standing at the desk with Ranika like they were the perfect fucking couple. When he saw me, his laughter dried up.

Before I could filter myself, I said, "My eyes gotta be fucking deceiving me, 'cause I know you ain't this fucking stupid."

I wanted to slap that damn smirk off that bitch's face and choke the fuck out of Jonathan. The receptionist was staring at me with her mouth open. I hated these bitches at work knowing my personal business, but they were about to have something to talk about now. "Jonathan, I'm 'bout to fuck you up."

I grabbed a pair of scissors from the desk and was about to lunge at him before someone grabbed me. "Ansley, I'm sorry. She had already picked a doctor here."

My chest was burning with rage. "Can someone get her out of here? I don't feel safe."

That bitch had some nerves. She wasn't safe. "Bitch, after I fuck him up, you next!"

Waiting clients were in shock as a couple of nurses hauled me out of the office. Since he'd attended previous Christmas parties with me, they knew who Jonathan was. So, no one was saying a word. When we got to the hallway, the doctor came out and fired me on the spot. I'd been working at this fucking office for seven years, and Jonathan fucked that up. How was I going to leave him without a job?

One of the nurses went inside and got my personal belongings. "I'm sorry, Ansley. He was wrong for what he did to you but flaunting it here at your job was heartless. I wish you the best."

Why was God punishing me? I refused to cry anymore over this bullshit, especially in front of these nosy-ass heifers. It was bad enough they'd seen my family unravel at the seams. Seams that were already strained to begin with. I grabbed my belongings from her and walked away, feeling disgusted, disgruntled, and in despair.

After getting in my car, my phone vibrated. I took it off silent mode, then read, *I'm so sorry.*

I wanted to throw that shit just as another text came through. *Hey Ansley. It's almost Christmas, and you've been on my mind. I miss you.*

Jayden had finally messaged me. Today wasn't the day though. I didn't feel like being bothered right now. Getting my emotions and attitude under control before it was time to get the kids was my main focus. I'd sent Jayden a few texts during our two-week hiatus to say that I missed him, but he'd never responded.

When I got home, I began packing some of my belongings. I knew after this, there was no way I could fake the funk anymore. That bullshit he pulled today had my insides turning upside down.

An hour later, Jonathan walked in the door. I heard his keys hit the countertop, then his footsteps down the hallway. He stood in the doorway, watching me box up some of my things. "I fucked up, Ansley. I'm sorry you lost your job. I'm gonna take care of y'all."

"Damn right, you will. I should stab you to death right now, but I know how much my kids need me."

He nodded, then left the room. Good for him. He could go be with that stupid bitch. I think she knew where I worked. She scheduled her appointment there on purpose to get back at me for chin-checking her ass months ago. She'd better hope we never crossed paths again, or I was gon' slap the shit out of her, pregnancy be damned. Sitting on the floor and leaning against the wall, I took three deep breaths to calm my nerves as I heard the door close. I guess he was going back to work.

I grabbed my phone and texted Jayden. *I missed you too.*

Immediately after, he called. I guess my plans of not talking to him today would be tossed out the window because I wasn't going to ignore him. "Hello?"

"Hi, Ansley."

"Hey."

"How have you been?"

I chuckled sarcastically. "There are no words for how I feel right now."

"What's going on?"

"I'm leaving my husband. When I met you in the park, I'd just found out that his bitch was pregnant."

"Damn. I'm sorry. That's fucked up. Is there anything I can do?"

"Nothing other than what you're doing right now."

"As Remo's friend, I'd promised him I wouldn't talk to you anymore."

"But?"

"He gave me clearance earlier today. I didn't want to disrespect him."

"I understand."

"So, what are you gonna do?"

"I'm packing some of my things now. I can't stay with him. I tried for the sake of my kids, but I need to be happy for them too."

"That's right. I'll help you in any way I can, Ansley."

"That's not your responsibility. Jonathan will take care of everything, voluntarily or involuntarily."

We continued to talk until it was time for me to get the kids from school and daycare. My life was in shambles, but the road to recovery was full speed ahead. There was no turning back, and I was anxious to see what my new life would have in store for me.

ix months later...

ANSLEY

"Why would you think it's okay to bring a whole baby in my damn house?"

"Because I'm paying for this house and every damn thing in it."

I rolled my eyes at Jonathan and crossed my arms over my chest. He took a deep breath. "I'm sorry, Ansley. I didn't come here to argue with you. It's my weekend with her as well as our kids. I couldn't leave her in the car."

"I'm sorry. Just seeing her is a constant reminder of the devastation of our marriage."

"Belan is innocent."

"I know, but how she came into existence isn't. It's hard for me to separate the two."

Jonathan's little girl was four months old. I eventually left his ass about four months ago, not long after Christmas. We had a huge blow-up at my parents' house Christmas day. I finally admitted to him as well as myself that it was the end. He'd done everything he promised he would do. He'd bought me a house in the west end of Beaumont and took care of all the bills, including food.

He wasn't in a relationship with Ranika. After he found out about her disdain toward me, he refused to be with her. Or so he'd said. Just as I'd thought, her choosing the doctor's office I worked at was intentional. He sat Belan's seat on the countertop and came closer to me. I looked up at him as he grabbed my hand. "How's everything been going around here? Are the boys giving you any problems?"

"No. Everything's been okay, Jonathan."

His acts of indiscretion scarred me. I still loved him, but I found myself not trusting anyone these days. Seeing the love he still had for me in his eyes, I turned away from him. "Ansley. I know this hasn't been easy. It hasn't been easy for me either. Seeing how I destroyed my family is depressing. Thank you for being a wonderful wife and mother. Even after you found out about my infidelity, you forgave me. I will never forget the love you showed me and how you took care of me and our children. I love you."

I took a deep breath and nodded my head. He was making me emotional as hell. I yelled for the kids. "Sage, Garrett, Alana! Your daddy's here." Looking back at him, I smiled softly. "Thank you, Jonathan. That means a lot."

"Do you still love me?"

Putting my head down, I nodded. When I looked up at him, I could see the emotion in his eyes. It was my first time admitting that I still loved him since we'd divorced. Our divorce was final two months ago. There was no fighting, so it went quickly.

The kids ran in the kitchen to their dad and hugged him. They were growing up. The boys had turned six the day our divorce was final, and Alana turned three in February. After hugging their dad, they hugged me, then grabbed their small duffle bags from the floor. Jonathan was staring at me as they did so until the baby started crying. "Well, I guess we better get going. See you Sunday."

"Okay."

"Bye Mommy!" the kids said.

"Bye babies. Have fun."

Once they left, I poured a glass of Stella Rosa Black and sat on the sofa. My life had been quiet. After I got fired, I didn't even try to find a job for the first three months. I started seriously looking a couple of months ago, but the market seemed dry as hell. Although Jonathan was taking care of us, I needed a job. There were things that I wanted to do for myself.

Before I could finish my drink, my cell phone was ringing. "Hello?"

"Hey, Ans. How was your day?"

"Hey, Jayden. It was good. How about yours?"

"Tiring. Remo let his lil position go to his head today, bossing me around and shit."

I giggled a little. Jayden and I had gotten close. We talked at least three times a week and sometimes went out. He wanted me to be his girlfriend, but I'd refused. Although I liked him a lot, I needed to discover myself again. We spent a little time together for Christmas, and we'd kissed. It had actually gotten hot and heavy once. After that, I refused to let it go there again.

He seemed to understand my standpoint. I'd been married and in love for a long time. I also had kids that needed just as much time to transition into this as I did. They couldn't understand why their dad and I needed to live separately. It was definitely hard to explain since they were so young. I think the boys had caught on though when they saw their dad holding a baby that wasn't mine. When he first introduced Belan as their little sister, they frowned at him. They knew I hadn't had a baby.

"Have the kids left yet?"

"Yeah, they left about thirty minutes ago."

"You wanna watch a movie?"

"Sure. You coming here? Or should I come to you?"

"I can come there if you don't feel like getting out. You sound tired."

"I am a little. Alana was extremely active today. Plus, I've started drinking."

"Aight. Say no more. I'll be there in about thirty minutes."

"Okay, Jayden."

I ended the call with a smile on my face. He was a good friend to me. I knew that Remo and his fiancée, Caricia, thought Jayden and I had more going on than what we did. Neither of us corrected them when they made their snide remarks about how much time we spent together, accusing us of fucking around. Just because they couldn't keep their hands off each other, didn't mean that Jayden and I were in the same place.

Caricia had just found out that she was pregnant, and I was supposed to be going with her to her second appointment. At her first appointment, they'd found out she was ten weeks. She and Remo had moved extremely fast. I guess when you know someone is for you, what's the point in waiting? I thought Jonathan was my one. It took him years to prove to me that he wasn't.

The knock on the door took me away from my thoughts. I grabbed my wine glass to bring to the kitchen for a refill, then opened the door for Jayden. "Hey, come on in."

He smiled and closed the door behind him, then made his way to me. As always, he pulled me in his arms and kissed my forehead, then my lips. I loved his lips. They were thick and so soft. "You want a glass?"

"What'chu drinking?"

"The usual, Stella Rosa Black."

"Yeah, I'll take a little. Not a lot, I gotta go to work tomorrow."

"Why didn't you tell me? I would have come to you."

"You know your needs come before mine, Ans. You sounded

depressed. I wanted to see you, but I knew you wouldn't feel like getting out."

I hugged him around his waist and laid my head on his chest. He always knew what I needed. He'd been so patient with me throughout this whole ordeal. "Thank you, Jayden. You always know what I need."

"Come on. Let's go sit down."

I knew he wanted a relationship with me, but he was sacrificing his needs for mine. He was putting what he wanted on hold, but for how long? Jayden and Caricia were best friends, and she told me that he's been wanting to settle down. She said that he liked me a lot. I knew he did. He'd just turned twenty-five, and here I was on the downside of thirty, a divorcee with three children.

What did he see in me that was so appealing? My stomach wasn't flat, that was for sure. I never wore makeup, and I rarely had my hair in a style other than a ponytail. Within the past six months, I'd probably gained fifteen pounds, and most times I had on sweats or tights with a long t-shirt.

After sitting next to him, he grabbed my remote and scrolled through the channels as I watched him. His smooth dark chocolate skin made me weak, along with his tapered faded and neatly trimmed beard. Those slanted, brown eyes always held me captive. When he glanced at me, I cleared my throat and averted my attention to the TV. Jayden knew that I liked him. I just couldn't dive in right now. While he seemed to understand, I hated feeling like I was stringing him along. He lifted his arm, and I leaned into him. I tucked my feet under me as he pulled me closer by wrapping his arm around me.

Jayden kissed my head and continued to scroll. Taking a deep breath, I relaxed against him, then took a sip of my wine. "What's wrong, Ans?"

"Nothing."

"You always say nothing. I can see that something is bothering you. Just say you don't wanna talk about it."

"I don't wanna talk about it right now, Jay," I said as thoughts of Jonathan invaded my mind.

"Is it about me?"

I sat up and turned to look at him. "I just feel like I'm stringing you along. I can't give you what you want right now."

"Am I complaining?"

"No, but..."

"No buts, Ans."

"Why? Why are you willing to wait for me? What happens if someone else comes along?"

"Are you saying you don't want me here?"

"I'm saying I don't want you sacrificing the things you want out of life for me. I'm still broken. Not as broken as I was six months ago, but still broken nonetheless."

"Ans, listen. Everything I want out of life includes you. I'm not giving up on you. We're friends, and I want you to be mine. I'm willing to wait for you." He pulled me back in his arms and kissed my cheek. "Now, let's watch TV."

ayden

I LAID IN MY BED, staring at the ceiling, thinking about my night with Ansley. She was everything I wanted. Her ex-husband had caused her self-esteem to sink so low though, she couldn't fathom that I would want her or a "ready-made family" as she called it. When I first laid eyes on her, I knew I wanted to get to know her.

Regardless of her current situation, that feeling hadn't changed. It had only gotten stronger. When she spent time with me for Christmas, I thought we were on to something special. She'd taken time away from her kids to be with me. We'd kissed, and it just felt so right. After that night, she pulled all the way back, only giving me bits and pieces of herself.

The day they filed for divorce she was so emotional. She'd come over while the twins were in school and Alana was at daycare. We'd kissed so passionately, and my hands had groped her curves, squeezing her gently as my lips blazed a trail to her neck and shoulders. When I slid my hands in her tights and grabbed her bare ass, it was like lightning had struck her.

She pulled away from me, apologizing over and over, then left. No matter how much I explained that she was who I wanted, she always came up with reasons why I shouldn't want her. She had some meat on her bones. I liked that, but she always said she was fat. Yeah, she'd gained a little weight during the divorce, but that only made her more appealing to me. She had ass for days, which I absolutely loved.

It seemed all the extra weight she'd gained had gone there. Then she talked about her stomach and thighs. I swore this woman was fine as hell. Those thighs kept everything warm. The one time she straddled me when we were hot and heavy, I thought I was about to die and go to heaven. It was so hot between her legs, I could've stayed that way for life.

She had three children, and her daughter was two years old at the time. I didn't care if her stomach was flat or not. She made it seem like she was big and sloppy. Ansley was only a size ten or twelve, but she said she was a six before children. So, on my off days, we went to the gym to work out and sometimes on the weekends when she didn't have the kids, we did so as well.

After watching a movie with her, I came home and laid in the bed. Whenever we spent time together, it took a while for me to go to sleep. My mind always tried to help me come up with more ways to prove my love to her. I had yet to tell her my true feelings for her because I knew she didn't feel the same way.

———

WHEN I DRUG myself to work and sat at my desk, Remo started in on me immediately. "Why you all quiet this morning? You and Ansley stayed up late last night?"

I didn't answer him. He was always on my back about his sister. Usually, I was the one that walked in joking, but 5:00 a.m. came early for me this morning after tossing and turning all night until one o'clock this morning. Finally, he sat next to me. "You aight?"

"I'm just tired. I left Ansley's sometime between nine and ten, but I didn't eventually fall asleep until around one this morning."

"What's going on? You stressed about something?"

I took a deep breath, then shook my head. I didn't really feel like talking about it. My mama had always said that I held things inside too much. I was her only biological child, and she said that I was just like my daddy. He'd disappeared when I was three. Neither of us had seen him or heard a thing about him since then. I tried to maintain my positive, playful attitude at all costs, but it was getting harder every day that I didn't have Ansley in my life as mine.

"Well, I'm going to check gauges. I'll be back."

I nodded then logged on to the computer. We were process operators at ExxonMobil. I'd been here for almost four years. Before I could get my programs up and running, I got a text from my stepsister. She was a couple of years younger than me. *Good morning. You at work?*

She was a student at TSU in Houston. She was in a summer session so she could finish her degree a semester early. I replied to her, *good morning, Cierra. Yes, I'm at work.*

Okay, call me when you have a minute. I'm not in class today.

I replied, *okay.*

Usually, she wanted to ask for money. I didn't have a problem with that though, because she was doing what she had to do to finish school. My mama and her daddy had gotten married when I was seven. So, we grew up as sister and brother, along with her biological brother, Daniel. Daniel was a couple of years older than me. I was right in the middle of them, age-wise. Their mother died from lupus about a year before their dad met my mama at the grocery store.

So, to say we were close was an understatement. Daniel and Mr. Jacobs taught me everything I knew about being a man and taking care of my mama and lil sister. Getting out of my thoughts, I stood from my desk to start my day, hoping my mind would leave me alone until lunchtime.

Just as I was heading inside to get my keys to go get something for lunch, Ansley sent a message saying, *Hey. Are you working tomorrow?*

Normally, she knew my schedule, but I was supposed to be off today. I'd worked a shift for a guy who had a funeral to go to. *Hey. I'm off. What's up?*

I'm cooking for you tonight.

Say no more. I'll be there after I shower.

She knew I loved to eat. As slender as I was, one would think I didn't eat a lot. I must have a high metabolism rate because I could never gain weight. She sent back, *lol.*

After getting in my car, I called Cierra. She answered on the first ring. "Hey, Jay."

She sounded down. "What's wrong, CiCi?"

"I'm pregnant."

Aww shit. "What?"

"I took a pregnancy test this morning. I'm so scared. How am I gonna tell Mama and Daddy that I'm pregnant?"

"Calm down, sis. You a grown woman. If you graduate in December, you'll only be, what seven or eight months? It will be okay. You know I'll help you."

She took a deep breath. "How could I have been so careless?"

"CiCi, don't do that. It's done now. Ain't shit you can do about it. Let's just move forward from here. Have you called a doctor?"

"Not yet. Jayden, I don't know if I wanna keep it."

"Why not?"

"Onyx doesn't want kids."

"Then he should have wrapped his dick up."

Now I was steaming. If he didn't want kids, he should have taken the proper precautions to make sure that didn't happen. "Jayden..."

"Naw, fuck him. How do you feel? Do you want to keep the baby?"

"Yeah. If I had been raped, that would be another thing, but I can't see myself killing my baby that I willingly participated in creating."

"Then keep it. Again, you know I'll help you financially and babysit on my days off. Mama would love having another grandbaby. She's been hounding me for the past year about it."

She giggled slightly. "Thank you, Jayden. So, what's up with you and Ansley?"

"Same ol', same ol'."

"Have you told her that you're in love with her?"

"Naw. I can't. I don't want her to feel worse than she already does."

"I hope one day she finally decides to give you a chance."

"Yeah, me too. Start researching doctors, so you can call and make an appointment on Monday. Let me know when it will be, and I'll go with you. Okay?"

"Okay."

"I have to go, so I can eat and get back to work. I'll call you when I get off. Call Mama and Daddy."

"I will. Love you."

"Love you too."

Whenever she was having issues, she always called me first. I suppose because we were closer in age. By the time she entered high school, Daniel was already gone. He went to the Army straight out of high school. So, we naturally became closer after he left, because I was the only one there. It helped that I always had a laid-back personality. I'd only been in two fights my entire life. Getting along with people was one of my strong suits.

———

AFTER SHOWERING, I headed over to Ansley's. I'd talked to Mama and listen to her go on and on about Cierra's pregnancy, then talked to CiCi to calm her down about Mama and Daddy's reaction. I needed some peace and Ansley always gave me that whenever I was near her. Although she was learning to be at peace in her situation, just knowing that she was allowing me to stick around gave me hope.

I understood where she was in her life, but she never forbade me from coming around, regardless of how she knew I felt about her. When I got there, Ansley was putting a bag of trash in her can. As I got out of the car, she smiled brightly at me. "Hey, Jayden."

"Hey. I hope you cooked a lot because I'm starving."

"You're always starving. Come in."

When I got close to her, I pulled her in my arms and hugged her, then kissed her forehead. She tilted her head up and kissed my lips, causing my whole body to react. Ansley grabbed my hand and asked, "What'chu think?"

She lifted the lid on the roaster pan, and I salivated at the site of those baked, pork ribs. "Damn, girl. That looks good."

"I knew you would think so. I know you love ribs."

"Thank you. Let's eat."

"Jayden, before we eat, I just wanted to apologize for last night. I'd just had a discussion with Jonathan, and I was still somewhat sensitive. Thank you for putting up with my mood swings."

I gently grabbed her chin. "I'm not putting up with you, Ansley. I'm feeling you. Everything about you. You know that. I love how passionate, sensitive, and emotional you are."

She hugged me again, and the heat coming from her was about to make me forget all about that food on the stove. I hadn't felt that from her in a long time. *Was she trying to tell me something?* Slowly, she moved away from me and grabbed two plates to begin fixing our food. All I could manage to do was stand there and watch her move around the kitchen. That wrap she'd tied around her body was gradually loosening. I licked my lips at what I imagined the sight to be underneath it.

I'd never seen Ansley naked, but what I imagined her to look like was enough to have me sweating. Sex had been nonexistent for me. Since I met Ansley, I hadn't entertained another woman. Well, I'd talked to a couple on the phone, but that was it. Everything inside of me craved, needed, and desired Ansley. Unless she physically and verbally told me to move on, I would be here patiently waiting for her.

She brought our plates to the table, and I was finally able to break my gaze from her. She'd cooked greens, macaroni and cheese, and cornbread to go along with those baked ribs. I licked my lips and sat down, ready to devour every morsel of food on the plate. Ansley sat a glass of lemonade next to my plate, then sat across from me with a bright smile on her face.

I loved to see her happy. Her light brown skin seemed to be glowing, and those thick, hot pink lips were taking my mind places it shouldn't be. I'd described her lips as DSL's to Remo before I knew she was his sister. Besides kissing them, that was the dominant image in my mind when I dwelled on them too long.

Ansley reached across the table and grabbed my hand, then blessed our food. Once she was done, I dug in. I'd eaten her cooking many times, so I knew exactly what to expect. She giggled as I closed my eyes and chewed my food. After swallowing, I looked at her until she looked back at me. "Ansley, this food is so good. Thank you."

"You're welcome, Jay. Thank you."

I watched her blush, then smiled and continued eating. "So, how was your day?"

She took a deep breath and shrugged her shoulders. "I guess it was okay. I still hadn't been able to find a job. I've put in tons of applications, but I haven't received any call backs yet."

"If Jonathan is taking care of everything, what's the hurry?"

"I just want to be able to do for myself, you know?" I nodded. "I haven't gotten my nails done in forever, and I've been doing my hair at home. I just want to sit at a salon and be pampered. Jonathan is already taking care of everything else. So, I feel uncomfortable asking him for more."

"You know, I wouldn't mind doing those things for you, Ansley."

"You aren't my man, Jayden. I wouldn't feel comfortable accepting money from you."

"I wanna be though. You do things for me all the time. Let me do that for you."

"I don't know, Jayden," she said, then looked down at her plate.

I shook my head slowly. She was so stubborn. I finished the rest of my food, then stood to take my plate to the kitchen to get more ribs from the pan. Ansley brought her plate to the sink as I headed back to the table. I ate my second helping of ribs while she cleaned the kitchen, softly humming. Glancing at her, I watched her hips sway at the sink and her curls bounce around her shoulders. Normally she wore a ponytail.

Had she gone through the trouble for me? I hoped not. She was beautiful, no matter what she wore or how her hair was styled. When I finished, I brought my plate to the sink and pressed my body against hers. She was washing a pot, and I couldn't help but wrap my arms around her waist. The way her body trembled made mine do the same. Slowly turning her around, I could see the desire in her eyes, and oh how I wanted to give her everything she craved. I lowered my lips to hers and kissed her softly, hoping she didn't stop me.

She lifted her wet, sudsy hands to my cheeks and pulled me in deeper. *Oh, fuck yeah.* I grabbed her by her hips and pulled her body into mine. Doing my best not to be too rough, I lowered my hands to her ass and squeezed. I'd been dying for this opportunity to present itself again. Her tongue eased into my mouth as she let out a soft moan.

My dick was hard as ever, and he was ready to pounce. It had been over six months since he'd dove into ecstasy. I lifted her and sat her on the edge of the sink, then tongue kissed her neck. "Ahh, Jayden."

Shit, her moans sounded so good. I lifted her once again and went to the couch as she wrapped those legs around me. When I sat, the heat that landed on my shit, was about to make me leak everywhere.

Ansley's eyes were closed as I gently caressed her ass and kissed her neck, then her shoulder.

I lifted my shirt over my head and began to slowly untie her wrap dress. She was grinding into me, and I was about to nut on myself. "Shit, Ans," I said softly as I looked at her erect nipples.

When I put my lips on them, it was like she snapped. Ansley quickly jumped from my lap, leaving me confused and horny as fuck. I stared at her as she put her arms over her breasts and picked up her wrap from the floor. *What the fuck just happened?* "I'm sorry, Jayden. I can't."

I stood from my seat and approached her slowly. "Ans, please. I'm practically at the point of no return."

She looked down at my jeans, then wiped her eyes. I hadn't seen her cry in a long time, and she wasn't about to let that happen now, either. Grabbing me by the waistband, she went to her knees. My eyes closed, and my breathing quickened as she unbuttoned my jeans and pulled my dick from my boxers. I opened my eyes to watch her spit on it, then she began stroking me. Not the release I had in mind, but I was grateful for what I could get.

I felt like a punk-ass nigga though. Allowing her to keep me around because I kept her company, was teeter-tottering on the verge of being used. My dick started to soften because of all the thoughts running through my mind. "Ans, you don't have to do that," I said, pulling her to her feet.

She looked confused for a moment, then her expressions softened. I pulled my pants up, then went to the kitchen to wash my plate out and put it in the dishwasher. "What's wrong, Jayden?"

Without turning to face her, I said, "Nothing. I'm cool."

She didn't push. I glanced at her to see she was putting food in the fridge, then went to the table. Taking $200 out of my wallet, I sat it there for her to have a day of pampering, then headed toward the back door. "Ansley, I'm gonna go."

"Jayden, please don't go."

I took a deep breath. "This is hard for me, Ans. I'm not trying to force you into something you aren't ready for, but if I stay, that's what might end up happening. I'll talk to you tomorrow, okay?"

She wrapped her arms around my waist, then said softly, "I'm sorry, Jay."

I kissed her forehead and broke away from her embrace. Slightly smiling at her, I left out the door.

nsley

"Why can't I just give in to him? I have strong feelings for him, but whenever I try to be intimate with him, I always think about Jonathan."

"You still love Jonathan, Ansley," Caricia, my soon-to-be sister-in-law said. "The question is, why are you hanging on to him emotionally?"

I shrugged my shoulders as she turned to look at me. Jayden probably hated me. I hadn't talked to him in three days, and it was tearing me apart. He'd left money on my table for me to get my nails and hair done. When I called to tell him 'thank you,' he wouldn't answer. I'd even texted him, apologizing and thanking him. Still no response. That shit hurt like hell.

"I don't know. I guess because we have so much history. Jonathan has been the only man in my life since I was fourteen. I loved him with everything in me, Caricia. It's like, I don't know how to love anyone else."

"You have to let go, Ans. I know you're afraid to try love again, but the only way you can fully give in to Jayden is to fully let Jonathan go."

"How, though? I see him every weekend when he comes to get the kids. How can I forget all the good times we had? Sometimes, I wish I wouldn't have been so quick to want a divorce. Besides the shit with Ranika, we'd gotten along amazingly well. That's why his infidelity came as such a shock to me."

"You and Jayden are my closest friends. I hate to see the both of you in such emotional turmoil."

"How is he?"

"Honestly, he's depressed. I think he loves you, but he'll never say as long as he knows you aren't going to give in to him. He did say he missed the kids."

Wiping my hands down my face, I sat back on the couch. When Caricia sat beside me, I rubbed her pregnant belly, although it was still somewhat flat. There was a small pooch that was barely noticeable. She had a doctor's appointment at one this afternoon, but I'd come over early and brought her some Zuppa Toscana soup.

She'd been having morning sickness, making it difficult to keep much of anything down. I told Remo that I would bring her some soup today. She grabbed my hand. "Just give him a try. He's been patient this long without a commitment. I know he would be willing to help you through whatever you're dealing with emotionally if you just let him."

I nodded, but there was no way I was allowing Jayden to enter my brokenness. He deserved more than I could give him right now. "Well, you ready?"

"Yes."

We both stood as her phone rang. I was sure it was Remo. He was forever checking on her. "I know, baby," she said, then giggled.

Just as I figured. We walked out the door, while she talked.

Jayden was in love with me? We continued on to my car and got in as my thoughts ran wild through my mind. Just as Caricia was getting off her phone, mine was ringing. I was really hoping it was Jayden, but it wasn't. Jonathan was calling. "Hello?"

"Hey, Ans. How are you?"

"I'm good, thanks. How are you?"

"I'm good. I just wanted to check on you and the kids. Y'all need anything?"

"I don't think so, Jonathan. Thank you."

"You don't have to thank me. What about gas? How much you got?"

"I'm on half a tank, so I'll make it to the weekend."

"You sure?"

"Yeah."

"Ans..."

I sat quietly, waiting for what he wanted to say. Caricia was staring at me as I took deep breaths. "Umm, I just wanted to say that I love you."

"Okay," I replied softly.

"I'll talk to you later. Tell Alana to call me when you get her. I have something to tell her."

"Okay."

"Bye baby."

"Bye."

This shit was torture! I ended the call. Why couldn't my heart just let go already? "You okay? Your face is extremely red, Ans."

My light complexion didn't hide a thing. I took a deep breath. "Yeah, I'm okay. Jonathan was asking if we needed anything."

"I applaud him for taking care of y'all. It doesn't excuse what he did to your family, but at least he's handling his responsibilities, plus some."

"I'm afraid that if I start dating Jayden, that's gonna stop."

There. I said it. Besides my emotional connection to Jonathan, I knew there was no way he would continue to take care of me if

Jayden and I were seriously involved. He knew that we were cool. That's it. If he knew we'd kissed and liked each other, he'd let go. The only reason he was taking care of us the way he was, was because he thought there was still a chance we'd repair what we once had. I could see it in his eyes, hear it in his words, and read it in his body language. His touch was gentle, and it reminded me of days when he would take his time loving me, cherishing me.

"Oh, Ans. Stop being so stubborn. Remo told you that we would help. Your parents said they would help as well. I'm so sure Jayden would help also."

"I can't do that. Y'all have a baby on the way. My parents are both retired. None of this is Jayden's responsibility. Let's change the subject, okay?"

She gave me a sympathetic smile. "Okay."

———

I'D KEPT the kids home with me this week since school was out. We'd been enjoying different activities all week. Honestly, I could use the company. I hadn't heard from Jayden in almost two weeks. Even after putting his money in the mail to him, he didn't call. There was no way I could spend his money like his heart didn't matter. I wasn't a user.

I'd finally gotten a call back from a doctor's office for an interview. When I'd gotten off the phone, I breathed out a sigh of relief. I was starting to think I had been black-balled until my old job called to say that they wouldn't disclose details of my termination and would still give me a good recommendation. They knew that I was placed in an unusual circumstance and would have never jeopardized my job intentionally.

After I got Alana ready, we were about to head out to the park. She was swaying her little hips in her swimsuit. "Umm, ma'am. Who do you think you are?"

I chuckled as I watched her frown at me. "Mommy, I'm pwetty! Daddy said so."

"You are gorgeous, my little doll."

She smiled at me and continued swaying her hips as she walked to the door with her towel. The boys were already there with their swim trunks and t-shirts on. I grabbed our picnic basket, then opened the door to find Jonathan standing there. "Hey. What are you doing here?"

"I decided to leave work early to spend some time with my favorite people."

The kids all yelled, "Yay!"

I smiled at their excitement. "Is there enough lunch in there for me?" he asked, looking at the picnic basket.

"Umm, no. Let me fix you a sandwich."

I sat it on the countertop, while the kids impatiently whined. He corralled them, then made his way to the kitchen. "You don't mind me coming, do you?"

"No, of course not."

"I wanted to spend a little time with them without having Belan. When I have her, she gets most of my attention. That isn't fair to them."

"Thank you for that. The boys often say that you barely got to play with them. I had to explain to them that Belan requires a lot of attention right now. They seemed to understand."

"Thank you, Ans."

I smiled softly at him because I knew he was trying. He'd always been a good father. Walking closer to me as I wrapped up his sandwich, he grabbed my hand. When I looked in his eyes, it felt like my heart skipped a beat. Before I could find my brain and wherewithal to stop it, his lips had met mine. The familiarity caused me to relax and close my eyes. When his hand touched my cheek, I quickly pulled away and wiped my lips.

"I'm sorry. I've wanted to kiss those lips again for a while now."

I didn't respond to him. Packing his sandwich, chips, and water, I closed the picnic basket and walked to the door as the kids jumped for joy.

We drove separate cars, and the boys opted to ride with their dad. "Mommy, you kissed Daddy."

I let the air leave me like a deflated balloon. Ignoring her, I turned up the radio and watched her excitement when "Can't Stop the Feeling" from the Troll Movie blasted through the speakers. Hopefully, that would make her forget about the conversation she was trying to start. I tried to forget about it myself and hummed along to the music.

When we got to the park, the kids were so excited. The boys took off their t-shirts and threw them at Jonathan, then the three of them took off for the water. I slowly shook my head as I giggled at their excitement. Jonathan helped me get their towels and the picnic basket from the car. We walked to a nearby picnic table and watched the kids play. "If I bring the kids to daycare Tuesday next week, can you get them?"

"Of course. What's going on?"

"I have a job interview, finally."

"That's good, baby. You know you don't have to work though, right?"

I fidgeted for a moment, then looked up at him. "Jonathan, I need to be able to provide for myself. You won't be able to keep taking care of two households. How will I move on?"

"I was hoping... praying that you didn't want to move on."

"Why?"

"I still love you. I know that you still love me."

"But I don't trust you, Jonathan."

"I know, but I was hoping that with time, you would learn to, again."

"Jonathan..."

Before I could finish my sentence, that bitch Ranika interrupted, "Oh, so this why you ain't answering your work phone."

I stood to my feet because I'd been dying for another opportunity to get at her ass. "I'm spending time with my family, Ranika. What do you want?"

"Oh, y'all a family again? You might wanna tell her that you still fucking me when it's convenient for you."

My eyes widened, then I slapped the piss out of that bitch. Jonathan tried to grab me, but I slapped his ass too. She stood there holding her face, then tried to lunge at me, but Jonathan grabbed her. He restrained her as I gathered our things. "Ansley, please. Ranika doesn't mean anything to me."

Right after he said that, she turned and slapped him while yelling obscenities. I went to the kids while they argued. "Come on, let's go. I'm gonna take y'all to a better park."

"Aww!" they all whined.

"Now! Let's go!"

They all ran to me, and I draped their towels around them and hurried to the car. After strapping Alana in, I could see Jonathan trying to break free from Ranika. I hurriedly got in the driver's seat and made sure the boys were buckled in, then peeled out of there.

ayden

"Foul!"

"Nigga that ain't no damned foul!"

I swear these weak ass niggas at the basketball court irritated me some days. He barely got slapped on the wrist, and he was hollering like a bitch. I'd been spending a lot of time at the basketball court. Tomorrow I had to go with my sister to her first doctor's appointment, so that would occupy my time.

It had been hell not talking to Ansley. She was all I could think about, and it was causing me to be overly fatigued. That's why I'd been playing ball so much. By the time I would get home and shower, then eat, I'd be so exhausted until the only thing I was fit to do was sleep. After I took the money from my mailbox last week, I knew we were most likely done for good. She'd stopped calling a few days ago.

Trying to get her out of my system proved harder than I thought it would be, especially after reading her text messages. I missed her so much, but I couldn't continue to hang around. Being hurt wasn't on my list of things to do. After the guys finished arguing, they settled it by letting him shoot one free-throw. Just as our game was about to resume, I saw Ansley and the kids.

Trying to act like I didn't see them was hard as hell, especially when she was staring right at me. Our team only had to hit one more basket, and our game would be done. The kids ran straight for the water spout, and Ansley followed them, carrying a picnic basket and looking like she'd lost her best friend. *Maybe she had.*

After one of my teammates sank a jumper, the game was over. Normally I would play two games, but I wanted to at least acknowledge Ansley and the kids. "Yo! You not playing again?"

"Naw. I'm done for the day."

"Aight. Holla."

I picked up my keys and phone from the courtside and hesitantly made my way to Ansley. She looked hurt and pissed at the same time as she rubbed her palms together. When she looked up and saw me approaching, she turned away from me. I swallowed hard. "Hey, Ansley. How you been?"

She didn't answer me. "Jayden!"

I turned around and saw Alana running to me. She threw her wet body onto my leg as I chuckled. "What's up, lil mama?"

"Nothing! Bye!"

She ran back to the water spout, joining her brothers again. Shifting my attention back to Ansley, I sat next to her. She scooted over on the bench. "Ans..."

"You've proven that I don't mean anything to you, so leave me alone."

"What? Are you serious?"

"Jayden, you haven't spoken to me in two weeks, nor have you returned my numerous phone calls or text messages. Well, I got the message loud and clear."

I took a deep breath and exhaled loudly. "Why can't you understand how much I want you? How much I need you! It's hard as fuck being your friend when I want and need more. You so hung up on that nigga, you can't see that I love you."

I stood from the bench and walked away. I should've just ignored her and played another game or went home. Telling her I loved her was my last-ditch effort at trying to salvage what we had. I had a female friend. There was no need for a second one. My whole purpose for approaching Ansley over six months ago was to get to know her and have a relationship with her. She knew that.

"Jayden!"

I'd gotten to my car and turned to see Ansley walking toward me. Meeting her halfway so she didn't have to stray too far from the kids, I answered, "Yeah."

"I'm sorry. I've had a horrible day."

She grabbed my hand in her warm hand, then my other. Shortly after she fell into my chest. I wrapped my arms around her. "What happened?"

Instead of answering me verbally, she held her palm out. It was extremely red. "I slapped the shit out of Jonathan and Ranika before coming here."

"Come on, let's go sit down."

We walked hand in hand to the bench she was seated at a minute before in silence. I could tell she was doing her best not to cry. She hated showing how vulnerable she was by way of tears. Swallowing hard, she continued, "Jonathan had surprised us by getting off early and coming to the house. We were just about to leave to go to the park, so he came along. While we were there, Ranika showed up. I don't even know why she was there or how she knew we were there, but she started shit with Jonathan about not answering his work phone."

"Aww shit. You been wanting a piece of her."

"Yeah. I stood as Jonathan told her he was spending time with his family. She really got pissed and pretty much blurted out how they were still fucking. I slapped the shit out of her, then him. What really made her words sting, was that for the past month he's been telling me how much he loved me and wanted us to get back together. He was just repeating it when she interrupted."

I blew out an exasperated breath and leaned back against the bench. *Why was she even entertaining that nigga?* She leaned back too and continued rubbing her palm. After sitting in silence, she called the kids over to eat their food she'd packed. Spreading out a blanket, Ansley sat their food there for them to enjoy, then sat back on the bench. "You want a sandwich?"

I twisted my lips sideways. She already knew I didn't turn down food. Slightly smiling, she dug out a sandwich and handed it to me. As I ate, she stared off, seemingly deep in thought. When I tossed the sandwich bag in the trash, Ansley looked at me. "Jayden, you said you loved me."

I nodded my head slowly, looking straight ahead. Looking into her eyes when she was feeling this vulnerable would put me right back in the situation we were in before. "Yeah. I've felt that way for at least the past three months. I gotta go, Ans."

"Please don't leave."

"I know you're hurting about what he did to you. I'm sorry for the pain you're feeling, but I need to go take a shower. I have an early morning."

"Okay," she said softly.

I stood and looked at her. "Bye."

"Bye."

My mind was saying get away from her as fast as possible, but my heart was saying something different. For now, I listened to my mind and walked away. When I got to my car, before I could get in, I glanced at her once again to see her head down. Hurriedly I got in my car before I yielded to everything in me that wanted to run back over there to her. Starting my engine and backing up, I took one last glance at her and drove away.

After arriving home, I immediately started the shower. I smelled like a damned skunk. Ansley had to be feeling horrible if she laid on my chest with me smelling like this. People always said that if you could smell yourself, then you *really* stank to everybody else. Getting within the confines of the shower, I grabbed my Swagger Old Spice shower gel. Ansley loved the way it smelled.

As I washed, the more my heart longed for her. It longed to make everything better in her world. To hold her in my arms and listen to her breathe. All of the things I'd become accustomed to for the last six months. Standing under the shower head in my marble shower, I allowed the water to erase my doubts and fears regarding Ansley.

After I'd eaten some leftover spaghetti that my mama had cooked for me, I grabbed my keys and gave in to my heart. I had to get to her. Now. Jumping into my Range, I headed her way and prayed that she was home. Holding her, kissing her, and comforting her wounded heart was all I could think about. She had a hold on me that I'd done my best to shake.

I turned in her driveway and saw her Traverse in the garage. She'd forgotten to put the door down. I walked inside of it and hit the remote, so it would go down, then walked to her back door. It was already eight o'clock, so she was probably getting the kids ready for bed. I didn't think about the time until now.

Ansley flung the door open, clearly ready to let somebody have it, but when she saw me, her facial expressions eased. She stepped aside and allowed me to come inside, then closed the door behind me. "Mommy! I clean!"

I smiled at the sound of Alana's little voice. Before Ansley could run away from me, I pulled her in for a hug. Feeling the tremble through her body made me just want to hold her forever. I let her go, so she could see about Alana, then sat on the sofa. Sage and Garrett came in the front room with their toy cars and was excited to see me. "Jayden! You wanna play?"

"Yeah! Where's my car?"

Sage jumped up and ran to the room. I knew them apart because he was a little thicker. Garrett was slightly on the thin side. "Why haven't you been coming over?" Garrett asked.

"I've been really busy."

I felt horrible for lying to him. Sage soon returned with a larger car for me, and I played on the floor with them until Ansley called for them. "Goodnight Jayden! Thanks for playing!"

"No problem guys."

They hugged me, then ran to their room. I sat there, trying to decide what I would say to Ansley. Not only did I want to comfort her, but I wanted to hear her say how much she wanted me. I needed to be one hundred percent sure that I wasn't wasting my time. I rested my head on the back of the sofa and closed my eyes, waiting for her to join me.

"Jayden."

My eyes opened slowly. I'd fallen asleep on her comfortable-ass sofa. That shit felt like it damn near hugged you. "My bad. I guess I was more tired than I thought. The kids asleep?"

She sat next to me and grabbed my hand. "Yeah."

We sat there silently for a moment. "You okay?"

"I will be. Thank you for coming. Umm, I need to tell you something."

I sat up on the sofa, angling my body toward her. One of my reasons for being there was to talk to her too, but my tongue seemed to be frozen in my feelings. "What's up?"

"I really care for you a lot, Jayden. Moving forward and leaving Jonathan in my past has been hard for me, especially since we have three small kids together. It forces me to see him. Not only that, but he provides everything for me. That's the main reason I've been trying so hard to find a job. I want to let go and try to move forward with you, but I know Jonathan won't continue taking care of me if I do."

"I understand you're in a difficult situation, but nothing would please me more than to take care of you. I have a five-bedroom house all to myself. You know that. Thanks to my deceased grandmother, I don't have a house note. My vehicle is paid for. If you truly wanna move on with me, we can make that shit work."

Ansley hugged me so tightly, it felt like she was cutting off my air supply. "I never wanted to make you think that I didn't want you, Jay. I do. I just didn't want you to think that I was an opportunist."

She released her death grip, and I coughed and rubbed my neck dramatically, causing her to laugh. I loved her laugh. "Ansley, the past six months, I've gotten to know how strong, independent, and caring you are. I know enough about you to know that you aren't an opportunist."

"I realized today that I was hanging on emotionally to Jonathan for my own insecure reasons. He's the only man I've loved. The only man I've made love to. I'm so scared to love again."

"Don't worry. I'm gon' treat you so well, you ain't gon' have a choice but to love me. And when you finally let me make love to you, I'm gon' make you feel like I should've been the only one pleasing this body." I lightly drug my fingertips down her arm, leaving goosebumps in their wake. "I love you, Ans, and I plan to show you every day if you give me the green light."

Her cheeks were red as a smile spread across her face. "Today, I realized that I was the only one unhappy. Jonathan has gone on about his life without me, although he tried to make me believe otherwise. I wanna be happy, Jay."

Bringing my hand to her cheek, I said sternly but in a deeper voice filled with desire, "So, let me make you happy, then."

She smiled again. "Okay. Well, start now."

She didn't have to say another word. I pulled her to me and kissed her as passionately as humanly possible. My tongue slowly found hers and started a dangerous dance. When I moved away from her thick lips, her eyes remained closed, beckoning me to take her hostage once again. The way her mouth parted turned me on so much. I kissed her neck and squeezed her thighs. "Jayden..."

"Yeah?"

"I can't wait to see what being yours feels like."

"Shit, I can't wait for you to feel that shit either."

nsley

I'D FINALLY STEPPED out of fear and took a leap with Jayden. That shit felt way better than I thought it would. I felt a sense of freedom. The way his mouth devoured mine was making me weak. It always did, but tonight, it felt different. Like he was holding back with me before. We'd made our way to my bedroom, and he'd taken off his shirt. I let my fingers trace the tattoos on his chest and arms, then kissed his lips.

Although I'd given into him and what I wanted, I wasn't ready for sex. Jayden being as attentive as he was, had sensed my hesitancy. After taking off his pants, he got in bed with me and pulled me to him. "I have to leave early in the morning. I promised my sister I'd go to her first doctor's visit."

"She's pregnant?"

"Yeah, and she's scared shitless. The dad doesn't want her to have the baby. I told her that I would be here for her and would go to her appointment with her."

"Okay. It's already ten, so you should get some rest."

"I should sleep well with you in my arms tonight."

I kissed his lips, then laid on his chest. Not even a minute later, my phone rang. I frowned. It could only be one person, and I refused to answer. "You need to get that, babe?"

"No. Only one person calls me this late besides you. You're here, and I don't care to talk to the other person."

He pushed my hair from my forehead and kissed me. "Okay. I love you."

"Jayden..."

"Relax. You don't have to say it back. I know how you feel about me, Ans."

I snuggled closer to him and gently rubbed his cheek. It felt like I should have been in his arms a long time ago. I draped one of my legs over him, and he grabbed my thigh, pulling it up to his waist. His eyes opened slowly as his hand inched higher. *Lord have mercy.* I was so turned on, but I would rather wait until we were alone. The kids didn't need to hear my reaction to him.

His dick print wasn't lying. I'd seen a long time ago what he was working with. Although I knew Jayden wouldn't hurt a soul, that dick was saying something totally different. I'd always heard that tall, slim guys never lacked in that department. Jayden didn't disappoint. "Ans, you so sexy."

"I'm fat."

"Don't ever say that. If you aren't happy with your size, I'll help you work out. But shit, this body is fire."

My phone started ringing again. I took a deep breath and rolled my eyes. Rolling over, I grabbed it to see Jonathan's number. Before I could decline the call, Jayden said, "Answer it."

I looked over at him, then hit decline and put my phone on vibrate. "No. I don't want to ruin tonight by talking to him. I'll talk to him tomorrow. I'm changing my 'do not disturb' time so it won't ring anymore."

I changed the time to ten, then locked the screen. Scooting back to his arms, he pulled my leg over him again. After kissing my lips, he closed his eyes. I stared at his facial features and what I loved about them. Those dimples and those damned lips were two of the best. Within ten minutes, he lightly snored, lulling me to sleep as well.

———

"Baby, I'm about to go."

My eyes opened slowly as I rolled over to see Jayden kneeling in the bed next to me. "Huh?" I asked groggily.

Looking at the clock, I saw it was only five in the morning. "I'm about to head to Houston. As soon as we're done, I'll be right back to you. Okay?"

"Okay. Be careful."

He kissed my forehead, then left the room. I laid there trying to get comfortable again as a little knock disturbed me. "Come in."

"Mommy, I had a bad dream," Alana whined.

"Come get in the bed with me, baby."

That was always her excuse to get in bed with me. She'd probably heard Jayden moving around. Out of curiosity, I looked at my phone to see Jonathan had called two more times last night. I rolled my eyes and pulled Alana in my arms. I didn't have to see him until tomorrow when he came to get the kids. We didn't have a court order in place, because I trusted him to take care of business. I just hoped I wouldn't have to file after I told him about Jayden.

When I woke up, Alana was still in my arms asleep. It was already nine. Slipping my arm from underneath her, I went to the bathroom and brushed my teeth, then peeked in on the boys. They were still out. I went to the kitchen to start breakfast. Just the noise from me moving around had awakened Alana. She came into the kitchen with a smile on her face.

"Good morning, Mommy."

"Good morning, sweetheart."

"Can I cook?"

I smiled at her and put her little apron on. She liked to help me put the biscuits in the oven. After we'd done that, I brought her to the bathroom to brush her teeth. Then, I made sure the boys were awake and getting cleaned up as well. When we got back to the kitchen, she sat at her little table and poured imaginary tea in her little cup from her tea set while I cooked eggs and bacon. My phone started to dance on the countertop. It was Jayden. "Hello?"

"Hey, Ans. I'm on my way back."

"Hey. How did the appointment go?"

"It went well. She's about ten or eleven weeks, and everything looks normal. She was thrilled when our mama called to listen in on the visit."

"That's great."

"What are y'all doing?"

"I'm cooking breakfast for the kids."

"Okay. I'll see y'all in an hour and a half."

"Be careful."

"Aight, babe."

I smiled and continued to cook. The boys made their way to the kitchen just as I plated their food. "Good morning," they both mumbled.

Since the summer started, they'd been sleeping later and later. I was still making them go to bed early, so I didn't understand it. I sat to the table with them and enjoyed breakfast. Right before I took my last bite, my phone started ringing. "Hello?"

"Well, well, well."

"Good morning to you too, Remo."

Jayden must have talked to him. Sometimes, I hated that he and Jayden were best friends. He was Caricia's best friend too, so if he didn't tell my brother, he was telling her. "Good morning indeed. How're my babies?"

"They're fine. They just finished breakfast."

"Good. So, is there something you might wanna share with me?"

I rolled my eyes. "I told Jayden that I would be his last night."

"Well, it's about time. Have y'all had sex?"

"You mean you don't already know that answer?"

"That's the only thing Jay won't talk about."

"No, we haven't Remo."

"Really? I always assumed y'all had been all this time."

"No. I'm not rushing into that."

"Good. What's on your agenda for today?"

"Well, first I have to have this conversation with Jonathan. I actually thought you were him. I slapped the crap out of him and his bih yesterday."

"What?"

"They're still messing around, but yet he's been trying to get me to take him back. She confronted us at the park with the kids."

"Well ain't that some shit. He didn't put his hands on you, did he?"

"No. I don't think he's that crazy."

"I hope not. I would hate for him to have to see me."

"Right. How's Caricia?"

"She's good. Still having morning sickness, but she's handling it well."

"Good."

"Well, I gotta go, Ans. I just had to call and mess with you. I'm happy for y'all, sis. If that nigga gives you any problems, let me know."

I giggled. "I doubt I'll have any real issues with Jayden. Thanks, Me-Mo. Have a good day at work."

"Aight, Ans."

After cleaning the kitchen and starting a load of laundry, Alana and I laid on the sofa to watch cartoons while the boys played in their room. Later on, we would go visit my parents. Briefly getting up to move the clothes from the washer to the dryer and loading another load in the machine, I joined Alana back on the sofa. I was dreading the phone call to Jonathan, but as soon as Alana fell asleep, I would call.

I woke up to a light touch on my cheek. Sage was standing over me. "Mommy, Alana's sleep and you are too."

He giggled as I smiled at him, then made a funny face. Standing to my feet and scooping Alana up, I went to my room and laid her in the bed, then kissed Sage on the forehead. I got the clothes from the dryer, then made my way back to the sofa. After taking a deep breath, I grabbed my phone and called Jonathan. "Hello?"

"We need to talk."

"Yes, we do. I'm sorry about what happened yesterday."

I grabbed a towel from the basket and began folding it. "Jonathan, I came to the realization yesterday, that I've been unhappy for months, almost a year. I also realized that for the last four months, I've been choosing to be unhappy. I've been hanging on to you emotionally."

"Ansley, I..."

"No. Let me finish."

"Okay."

"You've moved on. Regardless of how you say you feel about me, physically and emotionally, you left me a long time ago. I need to do the same. I met someone months ago, but I've been refusing to give him a chance because I've been clinging to the remnants of the life we shared. You are the only man I've ever loved. The only man I've ever been with. This was devastating to me, Jonathan, but I can no longer live in the devastation."

"Please, don't let go..."

"It's hard to hold on to someone moving in the opposite direction. I love you, but I love myself more. So, unless it's about the kids, don't call me. I know this probably means you'll stop paying all my bills, but I can't let that control me anymore. At first, I wasn't going to have this conversation with you until I got another job, but the time has been long gone for me to say how I feel."

"I'm sorry. Emotionally, I haven't moved on. It's just sex. I only love you."

"It's more than that to her, obviously. I haven't had sex since you. So, miss me on that."

"You're right."

"I wasn't good enough for you, but maybe I will be good enough for someone else. I'll never know that unless I'm good enough for me. I'm still broken, but in time I will be whole again."

"Ansley, I'm still going to help you, just as I have been until you start working. It's my fault that you lost your job. Everything is my fault. Okay?"

"Thank you."

"You don't have to thank me. Have the kids met this guy?"

"Yeah. He's best friends with Caricia and now Remo. They know that we are friends."

"I remember him. Is he your boyfriend?"

"I told him last night that I was ready. He's been trying to be with me for a few months now."

"Okay."

"Well, I have to go. The laundry is waiting for me."

"Okay."

"Bye."

Talk about a sense of freedom. This felt even better than last night. I took a deep breath, then continued folding clothes with a smile on my face.

ayden

I WAS a speed demon on the way back to Beaumont. Getting to Ansley and the kids was all I could think about. My sister's appointment had gone well, and she was so emotional, especially when she heard the baby's heartbeat. She said she couldn't understand how people could abort a baby after hearing that. I could agree with that, but everyone was entitled to their own beliefs and opinions.

Just hearing the baby's heartbeat had me all in my feelings so I could imagine how she felt. Mama was crying on the phone, making Cierra even more emotional. After her appointment, she wanted a breakfast on a bun from Whataburger for breakfast. When she got it in her hands, she was nearly salivating. I had to laugh because she looked the same way I did when I was happy about food.

When I turned in Ansley's driveway, I practically hopped out the SUV before putting it in park. A huge smile spread across my face when I knocked on the backdoor. Ansley was mine, and that shit felt amazing. I ordered her some roses to be delivered for tomorrow and planned to take her to dinner tomorrow evening after I got off. I had the envelope with the $200 she'd mailed back to me in my hand, so she could get pampered Saturday while I was at work.

She opened the door with as big a smile on her face as I had on mine. When I walked in, and she closed the door, I immediately hugged her and lifted her in my arms. She giggled and said, "Put me down, Jay."

I kissed her lips, then let her feet touch the floor again. Damn, she felt good. "Hey, Ans. How's your day been going?"

"Good. I cooked breakfast for the kids, I've done two loads of laundry, and I talked to Jonathan."

My eyebrows rose slightly. "Yeah? How did that go?"

"Better than I thought. I told him about you, but he still agreed to keep paying the bills until I started working."

"That's good."

"Yeah."

"So, I wanna take y'all to eat in an hour or so. You think they'll be hungry again?"

"I'm pretty sure Sage and Garrett will be. I wanted to go visit my parents later too."

"Where are the kids? Usually, they would have come in here by now."

"Alana is napping. She ate her belly full, then we laid on the sofa to watch cartoons. We both fell asleep. The boys are in their room playing."

"Okay."

I reached in my pocket and handed the envelope to Ansley. When she saw the outside of it, she knew exactly what it was. "While I'm at work Saturday, use that to get pampered."

She smiled at me, then hugged me. "Thank you, Jay. I really appreciate it."

"You're welcome."

"Mommy, I up!"

I laughed. That lil girl was something else. The cutest lil thing too. She was a miniature version of Ansley and her dad, Mr. Pierre. She came walking in the front room as Ansley laid in my arms. When she saw I was there, she yelled, "Jayden!"

"What's up, lil mama?"

She hopped in my lap as Ansley laughed. "Nothing! You know what?"

"What's that?"

"I think you oughta take us to McDonald's today."

My eyebrows lifted and I laughed. "Alana, really?" Ansley asked.

Alana shrugged her shoulders. She was too grown. "I think I can handle that. So, go get dressed. Tell your brothers to get dressed too."

"Yay!" she yelled, then kissed my cheek.

That lil girl was gon' have me weaker than wet toilet paper. She hopped off my lap and ran to her brothers' room. We laughed when were heard her yell, "We going to McDonald's!"

"You can't always let her have her way. She's got you wrapped around her pinky finger."

"That's my lil mama. I'm okay with being wrapped. You got me that way too."

She stood with a smile on her face as Alana came running back to us with a tutu on. I dropped my head and chuckled as Ansley said, "Oh no ma'am. Go back in the room." She directed her attention to me again. "We'll be ready in a lil bit, Jay."

I pulled her to my lap as she laughed. After tasting her lips, I let her up. She went to the back as my phone rang. "Hello?"

"Hey, big head."

"Hey, Reesh. What's up? How you feeling?"

"I'm good. I'm pissed at you though."

"Aww shit. What did I do now?"

"Why did I have to hear from Remo that you and Ansley were a couple now?"

Caricia and I had been friends for almost fifteen years now. Since sixth grade. So, whenever she found out something about me from someone other than me, she got mad at me. "I'm sorry, Reesh. I work with Remo, so it's easy to tell him things since I see him all the time. You don't have time for a nigga no more anyway."

She giggled. "According to what I heard, you ain't gon' have time for me either."

I laughed. "I'm at her house now."

"I figured as much. We oughta go on a double date."

"Yeah, we ought to. Y'all wanna go Saturday night?"

"That sounds good but let me check with Remo."

"Okay. Well, let me go before Alana kills me. I'm taking them to McDonald's."

"How sweet. Okay. Talk to you later."

Alana was standing there with her hand on her hip. Her hair was in two curly puffballs, and she still had on the tutu. I looked up at Ansley. "So, who's wrapped again?"

She laughed. "Oh hush."

The boys came from the back in jean shorts and t-shirts. "Hey, Jayden!"

"What's going on, guys?"

"Is it true you're taking us to McDonald's?"

"I don't know. Ask the boss." They immediately looked at their mother, causing me to laugh. "Naw. The boss is the one wearing the tutu."

They both frowned. "Lana ain't the boss. Mommy is," Garrett corrected me.

"I the boss!"

"Alright, lil girl. Watch your mouth," Ansley said.

I shook my head. "Let's go."

They all piled up in my Range Rover, despite Ansley insisting to drive at first. When we got there, they immediately wanted to go play, but Ans shut that down quick, fast, and in a hurry. "You can play after you eat."

After ordering our food, they had a seat while I waited for our order. My phone chimed in my pocket. It was my mama sending a text. *Can you come by the house?*

Yes, ma'am. After I bring Ansley and the kids back home.

Ugh. Okay.

I hated mentioning Ansley sometimes. She didn't think Ansley was the one for me, because of her children and failed marriage. She'd 'warned' that Ansley would eventually hurt me because her and Jonathan had been together so long. After I told her that Ansley was upfront with me about that issue, she started saying that Ansley was using me.

She'd never even met Ansley or the kids. I didn't want to bring her around until I knew she was mine. Proving my mama wrong would bring me great joy. I loved my mother, but she always thought she was right about everything. She'd insisted that I let my 'one' get away. Caricia. I had never been attracted to Caricia in that way. We were strictly friends, nothing more.

They brought our food out, and I made my way to the table. Ansley could sense that something was going on. I guess 'cause I wasn't smiling. I was always smiling, especially when I was around her kids. I loved kids. "You okay?"

"Yeah, baby. I'm good."

"Jayden call Mommy, baby," Alana said and giggled.

Ansley blushed, then said, "Hush girl. Here are your nuggets."

They all dug into the food as Ansley watched me. There was no way I could tell her about my mama, so I started smiling and joking with the kids to ease her mind. When there was a quiet moment, Sage looked at me, then Ansley. "Mommy, is Jayden your boyfriend?"

We both stared at him, Ansley with a surprised look on her face. "Yeah, he is. Is that okay?"

He shrugged his shoulders and said, "I guess so. But what about Daddy?"

"Your dad and I are no longer married. When we moved into another house, remember I explained that to you guys?"

"Yes ma'am," they all said.

It touched my heart. They seemed a little sad. "So, is Jayden our daddy now?" Sage asked.

"Jonathan is still your daddy. Nothing will change that. Okay?"

"Okay, but is Jayden gonna be our daddy too?"

I didn't know how to respond, so I left that to Ansley. If I had my way, I would be their step-dad, but I didn't wanna cause unnecessary drama. It was too soon for that. "Well, he's my boyfriend. So, we'll see. Right now, he's the same Jayden he's always been. Okay?"

"Okay."

They seemed to be satisfied with that answer. However, Alana caused the temperature to rise a lil bit when she said, "Nika said she wike our mom."

"What?" Ansley asked.

Her face was red as hell. She had to be talking about Ranika, Jonathan's baby mama. "Mama, Ranika said that we could look at her like our mama too," Garrett added.

"You only have one mother. Understood? She is NOT like your mama."

"Why not? I think she's daddy's girlfriend."

Ansley rubbed her temples. I decided to take over for her. "Look guys. You only have one mother and one father. Ranika is not your mother, and I'm not your father. They are the only two people you should call mama and daddy right now. Okay?"

"Okay."

Ansley was red as hell, and I couldn't blame her. I was shocked that chick had even met the kids. Obviously, Ansley was too. "Mommy, I'm done."

"Me too!"

"Okay. Go play."

The three of them bolted from the table to the play area. Ansley put her face in her hands. "I'm gon' really fuck that bitch up. I'm gon' start with that mutha-fucka first. When we had the conversation earlier, he said nothing about the kids ever meeting that stupid bitch. I don't want my kids around her ass."

"I'm sorry, Ans."

She grabbed her phone, but I pulled it from her hands. "Not now, baby. Wait until you're in private. You angry right now, and you might get loud."

"You right, Jay. I swear I could commit murder right fucking now. Jonathan really on my shit list. Shit starting to come out now. I'm gon' get more information out of them before I call him."

"When you mad, you become this gangster that I've never met."

"Shut up."

I smiled at her and pulled her close to me. She was so angry. Her body was trembling like a leaf. "I feel sorry for what he's gonna get tomorrow when he comes to pick up the kids."

"I don't feel sorry at all."

———

I DROVE in my mama's driveway and silently prayed that I didn't have to 'get smart' with my mama. Ansley was everything to me, and I'd go to hell and back for that woman. When I got out of the car, I slowly walked to the back door. I didn't have a good feeling about being here. My stomach was uneasy like some foul shit was about to happen or something. *Calm down, dude. You tripping.*

After my short pep-talk, I walked into the house to see my step-dad taking out the trash. "Hey."

"Hey, Jayden. How are you, son?"

"I'm good, Daddy. What about you?"

"I'm okay. How was my baby girl?"

"Nervous at first. After hearing the baby's heartbeat, those nerves subsided real quick."

He chuckled. "Yeah. I'm gon' call her a little later. Your mama in there. I'm about to take this out."

"Okay."

I walked to the den. Mama was sitting on the sofa watching TV, thoroughly engrossed. So much so, she never saw me enter the room. She was watching some movie on Lifetime. I walked over to the sofa and sat next to her, then kissed her cheek. "Hey, Ma."

"Hey, baby. How was your day?"

"It was good."

"Cierra is so excited, huh?"

"Yeah, she is. I videoed her. You wanna see it?"

"Of course."

I pulled up the video and gave her the phone. She smiled and pressed play as the tears rolled down her cheeks. "I'm so proud of her. I was upset at first because she's still in school. I wanted her to be established in a job before she thought about starting a family. But, there's nothing I can do to change it, so I might as well embrace her and get ready for a new grandbaby."

I smiled tightly. I could feel that she was about to start on me. "So, how was lunch with your ready-made family?"

"Really, Ma?"

"Jayden..." She took a deep breath and exhaled loudly. "What is it about her that is making you so head over heels? I don't understand it. She has three kids, and she's divorced. Not to mention she's six years older than you."

"She's everything I've been looking for. She's smart, funny, hot-tempered, loving, and kind. You would know that the moment you met her. She's beautiful, but her heart is worth more than gold."

She stared at me. I couldn't take it, so I closed my eyes as I continued. "Her kids are the most well-mannered kids I've ever met. Her daughter already has me wrapped around her finger. The twins are high-spirited little boys that love their mama. To watch how she's overcome so much hurt and the amount of courage she did it with only makes me love her more."

"Wow. I've never heard you speak of her that way. Well, let me meet her."

My eyes opened, and I gave her the side-eye and twisted my lips to the side. She slapped my arm, and I smiled. "Mama, she's my world."

"I see. Let me see if she deserves you."

"I sometimes question whether I deserve her."

 nsley

"WHAT IN THE entire *fuck* were you thinking, Jonathan? You let that bitch watch my kids? You have to be out of your gotdamn mind!"

I'd gotten to my parents' house, and they were too excited to see the kids. Before they could get settled good, they were ready to take them out again. However, I had to talk to them before they left. I'd brought them in my old bedroom to question them about Ranika. After I asked every question known to man, they'd gladly left me in my room to stew in my anger.

Shortly after, they left to go to Dairy Queen for ice cream. I took the alone time to call Jonathan's ass while I was still heated. That mutha-fucka had the nerve to say he left them with her once because he had to run to the office to pick up some paperwork he'd forgotten.

"Ansley, it was only for about thirty minutes."

"See, you must think I'm stupid like that bitch you impregnated. Sage said they watched Toy Story 3 while you were gone. The whole movie! You know I can't stand that bitch! She told *my* kids that they can look at her like a mother. What in the fuck were you thinking? Shit, you couldn't have been thinking at all!"

"Look. Lower your damn voice. You have my kids around a man that I've never been formally introduced to, but you have the nerve to come at me like that? As much as I do for you?"

"First of all, bastard, you cheated on your *wife* of seven years with that bitch. Then, had the nerve to bring her to my job, like I wasn't still your wife. I ended up getting fired from said job. You also found out that the bitch scheduled an appointment there on purpose because she couldn't stand me. After all that shit and history, you thought it would be okay to leave my babies with that hoe?"

"She's the mother of my child, Ansley. She wouldn't hurt my children."

"You know what? Don't come and get them tomorrow. I can't trust you to even make the safety of our kids a fucking priority. You would have done better taking them to your job with you if you weren't there that long. But you know what I think? You were doing some underhanded shit that you didn't want them to see."

"I'm coming to get my kids tomorrow."

"No, the *fuck* you aren't, and there's nothing you can do about it."

"I can stop paying them fucking bills, though."

"Then stop the shit! That goes to show you how much you think of your babies. I'm sick of you hurting and disrespecting me at every turn. We will move out next week. Fuck you!"

I ended the call and almost broke my cell phone when I slammed it on the table. How could he defend that fuckery? He knew it was fucked up what he did. He just didn't think I would find out. My boys were singing like canaries about that bitch. It took everything in me to act like I was okay with that shit in front of them.

Laying back in the bed, I closed my eyes and tried to calm my nerves. I would have to ask my parents if we could move in, just until I could get on my feet. The boys could sleep in Remo's old room and

Alana could sleep in the room with me. His ass was going to court. I'd be sure to file for child support tomorrow. *Bitch-ass mutha-fucka.*

When I felt like I'd calmed down enough, I went out to the front room and sat in my dad's recliner. I rocked in it slowly, thinking about having to uproot my babies again. Standing from the chair, I walked to my daddy's liquor cabinet and poured me a shot of Hennessey. I downed it, then poured another. After killing that one, my phone started ringing.

I snatched it from the bar. "Hello?"

"Hey, baby. I was calling to check on you. You okay?"

"Hell no. If I thought I could get away with it, I would literally go kill Jonathan right now. Jayden, he had the nerve to defend the shit. He left my kids alone with that bitch for over an hour!"

"Where are you?"

"I'm at my parents' house still. They took the kids for ice cream."

"I'm on my way."

"No. I'll call you when I'm headed home. I'm gonna ask them to keep the kids tonight."

"You sure?"

"Yeah. They shouldn't be too much longer."

"Okay. Call me when you leave."

"I will."

Just hearing his voice had calmed me somewhat. I went sat back down in the recliner and rocked until I'd fallen asleep.

———

"MOMMY, WE'RE BACK!" Alana yelled.

I opened my eyes slowly, and my mama immediately noticed that something was wrong. I swore, Thelma Pierre could read me like a damn book. "Ansley Malveaux, go to your room."

"Oooooh, Mommy, you in trouble!" Lana yelled.

I rolled my eyes as everyone else laughed, then headed to my room with Mama on my heels. She closed the door, then turned to look at me. "What's going on? I can see it all over you."

"Jonathan thought it was okay to let that bi... his floozy watch my kids."

I almost cursed in front of my mama. She hated when I used profanity. "What?"

"He left them with her for over an hour, and she had the nerve to tell *my* children to look at her as their mama. Then he had the audacity to defend his actions. I told him the kids wouldn't be going with him tomorrow. So, he told me if he couldn't get the kids tomorrow, he wasn't paying the bills anymore."

"Oh my God, baby. Well, you know y'all are welcomed to stay here. I wanted y'all here anyway. I always felt like if you did something he didn't like or if he got angry with you, he would use that against you. Y'all come home."

My mama pulled me in her arms and held me tightly as the hurt of the situation crept in. I swallowed hard and pulled away from her. Crying wasn't going to change this fucked-up situation. "Is it okay if the kids stay here tonight, while I try to start getting things together?"

"Of course, Ansley. For the record, you could have called her exactly what you were about to."

My eyebrows lifted. "What? You talking 'bout that bitch Jonathan cheated on me with?"

She smirked, then hugged me again. "God, I hate you're going through this, baby. You've always been my good girl. You didn't deserve this one bit."

"Thank you, Mama. The kids will be happy to know that they're staying tonight."

"Yes, they will."

She smiled at me, then we left the room. "Mommy! Did Grandma whip you?" Sage asked wide-eyed.

My mama laughed as my daddy chuckled. I rolled my eyes and shook my head. "No, baby. We just needed to talk."

"I didn't whip her this time," my mama said, then winked at them.

They laughed loudly, causing me to smile. They were the reasons for me keeping my sanity. "Y'all are staying here tonight, so behave."

"Yay!" they yelled.

I smiled, then kissed their heads, and hugged my daddy. "Mama will fill you in. Okay?"

"Okay, baby girl."

I left out the door and got in my car, then rested my head on the steering wheel for a moment. Grabbing my cell phone, I called Jayden. "Hey, Ans. You headed home?"

"Yeah. I'm backing out of my parents' driveway now."

"Okay. I'll meet you there, baby."

"Okay."

It only took me a few minutes to get home from my parents' house. Jayden turned in right behind me. The effects of that Henny were still lingering. I wasn't drunk, but I felt a little buzz. It was keeping me calm, though. So, I wasn't complaining. Jayden met me at the door and wrapped his arms around my waist as I unlocked it.

Once inside, he held me tightly against him and asked, "What did he say?"

"Paraphrasing, he said that she was his child's mother and would never hurt any of his children. When I told him that he couldn't get the kids tomorrow, he told me if he couldn't see his kids then he wouldn't be paying any more bills. I told him that we would move out next week and fuck him."

"Shit. He gon' make me fuck him up."

"No. You can't get involved in my shit, Jay."

"Yo' shit *is* my shit. Don't worry. I'm gon' take care of y'all and that mutha-fucka."

"Jayden. No. Stop. I need you to let me handle it. Okay?"

He refused to answer me or look into my eyes. I grabbed him by the chin and forced him to look at me. When he did, his lips crashed on mine. He kissed me with a sense of hunger that I'd never felt from him before, and I gave that shit right back to him. Roughly lifting me from the floor, he squeezed my ass like he was afraid it would get away. I wrapped my legs around him and he began walking toward my bedroom.

We crashed on the bed, and I lifted his shirt over his head and began tugging at his pants. He stared at me as I did so like he was in shock. I was slightly in shock too. Feeling him inside of me was something I'd imagined but never had the gall to go all the way. This argument with Jonathan had violently pushed me, and I needed the opposite emotion to level me out. It was time to stop playing with Jayden and being afraid to give my all to him, regardless of my past.

When I got his pants unbuttoned, then unzipped, I yanked them down along with his boxers. Grasping his hard dick in my hand, I began stroking it as he moaned softly. "Ans..."

I briefly let him go and lifted my shirt over my head. Unfastening my bra swiftly, I flung it to the floor and Jayden immediately latched onto my nipple, teasing it with his tongue. That shit felt so good too. He'd only seen me partially naked one time. "Ans... you sure? I don't want you to regret this."

"I'm beyond sure. Now shut up and come fuck me."

He quickly removed my pants and underwear, then spread my legs. "Damn. You don't know how long I been waiting for this shit."

He stood and let his pants drop to the floor as I scanned his body. I could see the muscle definition with every movement he made. He was slender but defined. When he got back in bed with me, he lowered his face between my legs. "Fuck, this is a beautiful pussy, Ans."

He'd never spoken so dirty to me, but I liked it. The moment his tongue touched my clit, I was sure I'd ascended into heaven. I arched my back, pushing that shit into him. "Oh, Jayden. Shit!"

He hummed on it, and I came instantly, coating his goatee with my juices and cream. "Damn, girl," he said, coming up for air.

Jayden wiped his hand over his chin and hovered over me. Maneuvering my hand between our bodies, I firmly gripped his dick and stroked it. He got on his knees, and I quickly adjusted my body, so his tip was right at my lips. Rolling over to my back, I opened my mouth and lightly sucked his balls. His moans were getting louder as I continued to stroke him. "Jayden put it in my mouth."

He looked down at me and tucked his bottom lip in his mouth, then hovered over me. When my lips touched his dick, I could feel him shudder. We stayed in that position for a minute or so as I teased his dick with my tongue. Rolling back to my stomach, I grabbed his dick and practically swallowed it. Jayden grabbed my hair and began fucking my mouth.

I looked up at him to find him staring at me. "Ans, I'm about to bust."

I applied more suction and kept a steady rhythm as his body tensed up. Massaging his balls with one hand and using the other to wrap around the base of his dick, I put in my best work. I made the slurping noises as Jayden cursed. "Fuck, Ans. Here it comes. Shiiiit!"

He released his load in my mouth, and I pulled away from it allowing some of it to flow out of my mouth down my chin. Jayden stared at me like he was taking mental snapshots of how I looked with his nut all over my mouth. Swallowing what was in my mouth, I wiped my chin on the sheets. As he recovered, I began playing with my clit while he watched. "Shit, Jayden. Come fuck me... please."

Jayden stroked his dick a couple of times, then rolled me over and straddled my legs. He pushed inside of me, and we both simultaneously yelled, "Fuck!"

Reaching around me, he gently grabbed my neck, then began stroking my pussy with so much passion, it felt unreal. "Oh my God. Jayden..."

"I love you, Ans."

His dick game was as good as thought it would be, and I was regretting every moment I had gone without it. Lifting my hips into him, he began stroking me harder and going deeper into my abyss of passion. Gently biting my shoulder, he released a growl that let me know I was everything he thought I would be too. Jayden gripped my ass tightly, then began giving me the fuck I'd been begging for. I wanted to climb the fucking walls to get away from him. That nigga was chin-checking my cervix with every thrust, making my arch collapse completely.

My body began to tremble, summoning my orgasm. "Give it to me, Ans. Cum on my dick, baby."

I screamed out every drop as that shit shot through me like water through a compromised dam. My muscles were contracting around his dick, squeezing him like she didn't want him to leave. "Fuck!" he yelled.

He gave me one final thrust, then laid his body on top of mine, resting on his forearms. Littering my neck and shoulders with kisses, he whispered in my ear, "That was good as fuck."

He rolled over, then laid next to me and pulled me close. After we were silent long enough, he asked, "So, what are you going to do?"

"I'm gonna move in with my parents."

ayden

"WHAT?"

"I'm moving in with my parents."

"Why, when you and the kids can move in with me?"

"Jayden, it's too soon. Please understand. It's not about us. It's about what's best for them."

"I suppose I understand that."

I couldn't believe we'd had sex. That shit was so good, I wanted to scream like a bitch, especially when them DSL's finally wrapped around my shit. No more imagining, that shit had happened. I needed a fucking cigarette, and I didn't even smoke. It had been a long time coming. I just hoped her hasty decision to let me inside that hot box didn't come back to bite me in the ass.

That had caught me totally off-guard and unprepared. I didn't wear a condom, so I hoped she was on the pill. There was no way I was letting this moment pass me by. Since she didn't ask if I had one, I assumed it didn't matter to her. Then again, she probably hadn't used one in forever and didn't even think about it. I could definitely tell she hadn't had sex in a while. Her pussy was so tight, it was impossible to divert my nut for any longer than I did.

After the first two or three strokes, I could feel that shit rising to the surface. I'd had to think about anything but what was going on at that moment just so it would last longer. Eight months without sex was the longest I had ever gone. When I met Ansley, it had been almost a month since I'd gotten any.

She was laying on my chest, playing with my nipple. My shit was rising to the occasion again. "Ans, unless you ready to be fucked again, I suggest you stop."

"Who said I wasn't?"

I roughly pinned her on her back to the bed. She was staring at me with those sexy, slanted, brown eyes. My dick sprang into action the minute she licked those thick, soft lips. Damn. My dick sniffed out that opening and dove inside. Closing my eyes, I slowly lifted her leg to her shoulder as she moaned. Fuck, sex was so good with her. I was sure it had a lot to do with how much I loved her too. Rarely were my emotions involved during sex until now.

"Shit, Ans."

She pulled my face to hers and kissed me deeply, and I slowly continued to stroke her. My whole body was hot. Felt like a furnace was sitting on my back. Rolling over, I pulled her on top of me. I caressed her titties as she began her ride, pulling my shit to the surface. She leaned over to kiss me, and I grabbed her ass as she slowed her pace. Fuck this was torture.

Sitting back up to continue her ride, I sat up with her and held her tightly around her waist. She was making me extremely sensitive. "Ans, you know this shit all yours, right?"

"I was hoping so, Jay. You feel all this hot, wet goodness on you? That's all yours too."

"Fuck. I'm gon' live here too, baby."

"Pleeease do... Ahh. I'm cumming!"

The way that pussy shot that out, she wasn't gon' be able to sleep in this bed tonight. Everything was wet. When the wave had subsided, I threw her to the bed and rolled her to her stomach. Entering her from the back, I watched her ass jiggle as I pounded that wet pussy repeatedly while she screamed my name. I slapped her ass cheeks and watched them jiggle for me, then really went to work. My shit was trying to bust through to that uterus to plant my seed right where it needed to be. No traveling necessary.

"Jayden! Fuck!" she screamed.

"Yeah, Ans. I love your pussy."

"I'm cumming again... Oh, fuck!"

Her pussy had become a damned faucet when it erupted, and I loved that shit. It let me know that I was doing my job. I slid my thumb in her asshole and watched her squirm. She started moaning even more so I could tell she'd gotten comfortable with it. As I fucked both holes, I closed my eyes and grabbed her hip, pulling her into me.

"Fuck, I'm 'bout to nut, Ans."

She jerked away from me, then turned around and put her mouth on it. *Oh, fuck!* She was a damned freak, and I'd hit the fucking jackpot. I growled out, "Fuuuck!" I bust in her mouth as she sucked me dry. "Ansley, shit!"

I literally had to push her off it. She laid back in the bed with a satisfied grin on her face, and I collapsed next to her. My heart was beating so damned fast, it seemed I couldn't catch my breath. She rolled into me and asked, "You okay?"

"Hell yeah."

She giggled. After a couple of minutes, she got up and went to the bathroom. She started the shower, then walked back into the bedroom. "Stop, Ans."

She stopped mid-stride. "What?"

I licked my lips. "I just wanna admire your body. We dove right in, and I didn't get to really focus on how perfect you are. Damn."

She blushed as I looked her over from head to toe and back. The way she cowered under my gaze only made me love her more. She was so confident and assertive in the bed, but the total opposite otherwise. Lady in the streets but a freak in the sheets. I'd heard that saying my whole life, and now I saw it personified in Ansley. "C'mere, baby."

She made her way to me, then sat in the bed next to me. "So, how will I properly date you if you're living with your parents?"

"The same way you date me now. It's not like you've never met them. Only when we want to engage in these types of activities, we'll have to go to your place."

I pulled her closer. "I love these types of activities. Damn."

She blushed again. "Me too. Let me shower."

"Right now? I'm just gonna get you dirty again."

"Then I'll shower again. I'm a sticky mess."

I chuckled. "Me too."

"Well, come with me then."

"It's gon' be a long shower, Ansley. You done gave me a taste. Now I'ma be like a stray cat. You ain't gon' be able to get rid of me."

"Why would I wanna get rid of you, Jayden?"

"Well, damn, baby. Say that shit."

She giggled, and we made our way to the shower.

———

AFTER HELPING Ansley clean her bed and wash sheets, I watched her start packing the kids' clothes and toys. The anger had found its way back to her and had penetrated her every movement. She threw clothes into garbage bags and bins. As she filled them, I brought them outside to her Traverse. I couldn't wait to talk to Remo about that shit that bitch-ass nigga had done. As soon as I could think of something, I was coming for his ass.

When Ansley got done packing the kids' clothes, she began packing some of hers. Honestly, I was glad she was moving out. Him paying her bills was keeping him too involved with her. He was front and center. Now, the way he did that shit was foul, but nevertheless, he was a done deal until it was time for him to get the kids. I sat on the floor next to her as she packed and kissed her shoulder.

"Why was I so naïve? None of this stuff is in my name, not even my phone. So, if he wanted to cut that shit off, he could."

"Well, we'll have to fix that tomorrow. We can go to Verizon or wherever you wanna go, and you can get your own wireless plan."

I kissed her head as she looked up at me. "Jayden, I only have a couple of grand left in my account."

"Okay. And?"

"I'm gonna wait to see if he cuts it off before I get another one."

"I'm gonna pay for it, Ansley. At first, I was gonna suggest adding you to my account, but I knew you wouldn't go for that after what you just said."

She leaned against me, and I kissed her head. "Jayden, I pray every day that God won't allow me to be stupid. I have three little ones to look after. I prayed that He helps me to be the best mother I can be. My kids are everything to me, and I don't want them to have to ever go through crap like this again. All the moving, my mood swings, the arguing, and fighting. It's just been a lot."

"I know it has, babe. Look at me." She lifted her head and stared in my eyes. They looked so sad. "I will never, *ever* do anything to jeopardize the kids' mental health or yours. I wanna take care of y'all, but I can only do that if you let me." I gently rubbed her cheek, still staring into her sad eyes. "You have to let me, Ans."

"I know," she whispered as she dropped her head.

I lifted it by her chin. "You gon' let me?"

"I'ma try, Jayden."

"Really?"

"Yes, really. But baby steps, okay?"

"Okay."

I kissed her forehead again, then helped her continue packing her things.

I had to go to work in the morning, so I left Ansley around nine to go get cleaned up and go to bed. She'd air-fried us some chicken, and we'd made love again before I left. If I wasn't hooked before, I was definitely hooked now. I didn't know how I was gonna get any sleep without her in my arms tonight.

nsley

"Girl, when the last time you got your hair done?"

"It's been at least eight months."

"I knew I hadn't seen you in a long time. What's the occasion?"

"No occasion. I just wanted to be pampered."

There was no way I was about to tell these messy bitches in here any of my business. They gossiped about everybody, and the minute I left, I would be next on the list. I only came here because Tara could do the hell out of some hair. She was a beast with it.

Yesterday, Jayden had flowers delivered to my house, and they were gorgeous. It was the largest bouquet of roses I'd ever seen. I hadn't seen him since Thursday night, and my body missed the hell out of him. When he got home, he called me to tell me goodnight once again, and how much he enjoyed having me. I'd reciprocated the sentiment. Yesterday, he was exhausted after work, so he didn't come over, but we talked on the phone for an hour. I'd gone and got another phone without him, but he insisted on paying me back when he saw me today.

Jonathan's ass had the nerve to call yesterday to see if I had changed my mind about letting him get the kids, which incited another argument. For the first time ever, he called me out of my name, and I wanted to go through the fucking phone. I'd called Ranika a bitch, and this nigga said, "If she's a bitch, then so are you."

My hands were itching for the rest of the night because I was doing my best not to catch a case. I wanted to slow roll up on his ass and just start shooting. Good thing I didn't own a gun, because he would have been a dead mutha-fucka. I couldn't believe he called me a bitch. When Jayden had called, I couldn't even answer the phone initially. I had to call him back. There was no way I was gonna tell him what Jonathan called me though. I'd just told him I was arguing with Jonathan about him seeing the kids.

When I left the hair salon, I headed home to change into the only outfit I still had there. I decided not to even wait until next week. The kids had been enjoying time with my parents this weekend. It allowed me time to get everything packed up and moved. When I told them we were moving in with Grandma and Grandpa, they were beyond excited.

After getting changed into my somewhat form-fitting skirt set and putting on make-up, Jayden was knocking at the back door. We were going on a double date with Remo and Caricia. I hadn't seen either of them since her last appointment. However, moving in with my parents, I would be seeing them a lot more. When I opened the door, his mouth fell open. "Damn."

"What?"

"You look amazing."

"So do you."

I lightly kissed his lips, then took the small bouquet of lilies from him. I put them in water, then turned to find him staring at me. He looked damn good in his electric blue pants and vest. He wore a long-sleeved black shirt with it and some black dress shoes. When my eyes met his again, I reiterated what he said. "Damn."

He smiled, flashing those beautiful teeth and deep-ass dimples. I was glad I wore black. We hadn't even discussed what either of us was wearing, only that we would be dressy. "I take it that you like my ensemble."

I pulled him to me by grabbing his vest. "You look sexy as hell, Jay. Do we have to go to dinner?"

He chuckled, then spun me around, holding me close to him. "Don't start. I'll call Remo right now, then mess up this beautiful hair you sat at the salon for hours to get styled."

"Well, we better go then, because that magic wand in your pants is starting to hypnotize me. I don't feel like hearing Remo's mouth."

He softly kissed my neck and moved his hands to my breasts. I'd missed his touch, and I already couldn't wait for the date to be over. "Come on, baby."

I grabbed his hand and was walking toward my bedroom when he burst into laughter. "Oh, you meant we needed to leave. My bad."

I laughed along with him, then grabbed my purse and my bag. Looking around the house once more, I followed Jayden out, then locked the door. He escorted me to his Range, and we headed to The Grill for our seven o'clock reservations. While in route, Jayden grabbed my hand. "So, are you nervous about your interview Tuesday?"

"Not at all. Hopefully, that doesn't change. I hadn't really been thinking about it."

"I'm sure you'll get it. You're good at everything you do," he said seductively.

My face heated up as I glanced at him. "Thank you."

He was grinning from ear to ear. It felt good to know how happy I made him. When we drove in the parking lot, I saw Remo helping Caricia from the car. Remo and I didn't look a thing alike. He looked like our mother; milk-chocolate complexion, flat nose, thin lips, and somewhat beady eyes. I looked like my father; light-brown skin, pointy nose, thick lips, and slanted eyes. Whenever we went some-where together, people thought we were a couple.

Jayden parked, then got out and helped me out. I didn't notice the crack in the cement and fell right into his arms. "You okay?"

"Yeah."

We stared into one another's eyes, and I lifted my hand to rub his cheek. Someone clearing their throat got both of our attention. "Y'all can gaze lovingly into each other's eyes another time. Let's go eat."

I rolled my eyes at Remo and kissed Jayden's cheek, then wiped the lipstick off it. "Y'all look so good together. Hey sis," Caricia said.

"Hey," I said, then lightly hugged her.

She looked good in her wide-legged dress pants and form-fitting shirt, showing off her little baby bump. Jayden and Remo shook hands, then I hugged him. "Hey, sis."

"Yeah, yeah. Hey."

We all walked inside, and the hostess escorted us to our table. Once we sat, Remo asked, "So, how have you love birds been?"

"Remo, you act like you're the older brother. You do realize I'm almost five years older than you, right?"

He chuckled. "It's fun to give you a hard time, Ans. How long we been doing this?"

"Along twenty-six years."

He chuckled then picked up the menu as Caricia said, "Well, we have prospect baby names."

I sat my menu down and looked at her, propping my chin on my hand. "We haven't come up with a middle name for the girl yet. We can't seem to agree on anything. If it's a girl, we will name her Teagan. If it's a boy, we'll name him Grayson Night Pierre."

"Those are cute names, Caricia. I'm glad you didn't name the boy a junior. Giving him Remo's middle name was good enough."

"Hush, Ansley. I didn't want a junior, anyway."

We continued to enjoy the rest of our dinner. My salmon with mushroom sauce drizzled over it was so delicious. Jayden had gotten steak and an etouffee. I really didn't know where he put all the food he ate. As we finished up, my cell phone was ringing. It was someone from my parents' house. That immediately made me nervous. "Hello?"

"Ansley, I had to call the police on Jonathan."

"What?"

"He came here to try to take the kids. I called the police on him for trespassing. The kids are distraught."

"Shit. I'm on my way, Daddy."

Everyone was staring at me as I got off the phone. Before I could speak, the waiter brought our tickets. As soon as he walked away, all eyes were back on me. "Jonathan tried to take the kids. I need to get back to Mama and Daddy's house. The kids are upset."

Caricia's hands flew to her mouth as anger surged through Remo. He'd *been* wanting a go at Jonathan. Jayden dropped $90 on the table, and said, "Let's go."

Remo and Caricia were right behind us, and once we got outside, I started running in my heels to get to Jayden's Range. All I could think about were my babies. I could vaguely hear them in the background while I was on the phone with my daddy. When we got in the vehicle, I immediately called Jonathan's ass. He didn't answer the phone. *Ugh!*

I wanted to go to the house so bad, but my children needed me. Jayden took the usual ten minutes to their house down to seven. Not waiting for him to open my door, I hopped out and ran inside the house. Alana was lying on my mama's lap. As soon as she saw me, she hopped off and ran to me.

I lifted her in my arms and hugged her tightly. "Mommy, Daddy was mad. He was yelling."

"Don't worry, sweetheart. Everything's gonna be okay."

Sage and Garrett came to the front room as Jayden, Remo, and Caricia walked in the door. "You okay, boys?"

"We don't wanna ever go with Daddy again. He was mean to Grandpa."

I went to the sofa, and the boys sat on either side of me as I closed my eyes. Why was he tormenting my children and me? Opening my eyes, I saw Caricia hugging Sage and Mama hugging Garrett as Jayden, Remo, and Daddy went outside. Monday, first thing, I would be at the Attorney General's Office.

Alana had finally gone to sleep, and I was exhausted. I laid her in the bed, then brought the boys to their room. "Mommy, why was Daddy mean to Grandpa?" Sage asked.

"I don't know why he was mean to Grandpa, but he's angry with me. I fussed at him about something he did wrong. So, I told him until he made that right, y'all couldn't go to his house. I'm sorry boys. I feel like I put y'all in the middle of our drama."

The tears I was desperately trying to hold in, fell down my cheeks. They both hugged me. "It's okay, Mommy. Don't cry," Garrett said, trying to comfort me.

"I love y'all. Come on, get in bed."

"Love you too, Mommy."

I tucked them in, then left the room to find the men had all come back inside. Jayden stood and walked to me. He pulled me in his arms and hugged me tightly. When I pulled away, he wiped the tears from my eyes, but he didn't say a word, neither did Daddy or Remo. I sat on the sofa and took a deep breath.

I wanted to call Jonathan's bitch-ass again, but I couldn't have that conversation in front of my parents. My babies were so hurt and seeing them that way crushed me beyond words. Jayden sat next to me and pulled me in his arms once again. "Well, we gotta go, sis. If you need anything, let me know."

Remo was extremely short, and I knew it was because he was angry. When he got that upset, he always quieted down, especially in front of our mama. He hugged me, then mama, and Caricia did the same. Mama kissed my head, then smiled at Jayden. "I'm going to bed, baby. We'll talk tomorrow, okay?"

"Okay, Ma. Thank you."

She kissed Jayden, then my daddy shook his hand. Daddy hugged me and said, "Goodnight, princess."

Whenever he knew I was hurt as an adult, he called me princess. He always called me that growing up. So, whenever I was hurting or he was feeling sensitive toward me, I was his little girl again, no matter how old I had gotten. Once they'd gone to their room, I turned to Jayden. "Thank you for being here for us. I know you have to get up early, though. I'm sorry that bastard ruined our night."

"Ans, it's my job to be here for you and the kids. I love you, and I love them. I wish I could stay with y'all."

I kissed his lips, then said, "Come on. It's already almost eleven."

He stood from the couch, and I could tell he was tired. I grabbed his hand and escorted him to the door. He turned to me and gently kissed my lips. Before he could leave, Alana was walking back up front. "Bye, Jayden."

"Bye, lil mama. Come give me a hug."

Alana ran to him, and he picked her up and held her tightly. "Jayden? Are you gon' be my daddy?"

I watched him swallow hard. He glanced at me as if he wanted me to respond, but I didn't say anything. "I'll be whoever you want me to be. Okay?"

She smiled. "What if I want you to be Mr. Incwedible?"

He chuckled. "Then that's who I'll be. I guess I need to get a super suit made, huh?"

She giggled, then he set her on her feet. He grabbed my hand as I smiled at him. "Call me when you get home, so I know you made it safely."

"Okay."

He looked down at Alana to see she wasn't paying attention to him, then mouthed, *I love you.*

I hugged him tightly and kissed his cheek. After he left, Alana and I went to the room. I got undressed, then went to the bathroom to clean my face. I'd take a shower in the morning. My baby needed me. As I wiped the makeup off, Alana said, "Mommy? Daddy was mean."

"Try not to think about that anymore. Okay, sweetheart? I know it's hard, but can you do that for me?"

"Okay, Mommy."

"I love you."

"I love you too, Mommy."

We got in the bed, just as Jayden called. He called on my new number. "Hello?"

"Your other phone is off now."

I rolled my eyes in frustration. "Okay. Get some rest."

"Okay. Text me when you wake up. I love you, Ans."

"Okay, Jay. Talk to you tomorrow. Thanks again."

I ended the call and pulled Alana in my arms. She snuggled into me as I stared at the wall, hoping things didn't get worse before they got better.

ayden

RAGE SURGED through me the entire night, and that made going to sleep almost impossible. Fucking Jonathan up was all I could think about. I'd never been in a situation like this before. Usually, it took a lot to get me this angry, but lately, this nigga had been tap dancing on all my buttons. Ansley and the kids were my buttons. Last night was especially hard. Seeing how upset the kids were caused rage to infiltrate my very core.

Remo and Mr. Pierre weren't any better. We were outside trying to come up with a plan to make him pay for the trauma he'd put the kids through. Going after his job wouldn't benefit the kids. We'd looked up their ethics policies, and his latest behaviors had violated one or two bullets. The first course of action would be a suspension. If the situation wasn't rectified, then he would be terminated. So, him being jobless would mean that he couldn't be a financial help to Ans and the kids.

I sat at work in a funk along with Remo. His eyes were as puffy as mine and besides us speaking, we hadn't said anything else to anyone or each other. My phone vibrated, so I took it from my pocket to see a good morning text from Ansley. *Good morning, Jay. I'm just waking up. I hope your day has been good so far.*

It was only eight, but I'd already been here for two hours. I texted her back. *Good morning, Ans. I'm a little tired, but I'm good. I can't wait to see y'all when I get off.*

"Jay, I think I got something."

"Something that ain't gon' hurt Ans and the kids or get us in trouble, right?"

"Right. I know this dude that work up here. When I got here this morning, I overheard him talking about a chick named Ranika. Ain't that Jonathan's baby mama's name?"

"Yep."

"He was talking 'bout how he wanted to fuck her, but he thought she might have a man."

I chuckled. "So, you gon' send him after her?"

"Yep."

"Well, that's minor, but that should ruffle his feathers a little bit."

"Yep, but it could lead to more. I just got to get the ball rolling. Leonard always eats lunch in the breakroom, so I'm going in there today too."

I chuckled again as my phone vibrated again. *I'm sorry you're tired. Why don't you go home and get some rest when you get off?*

Ansley just didn't get it. *Because I won't rest until I see y'all.*

She sent back a kiss emoji. I slid my phone in my pocket, then went outside to check gauges.

When I got off, I went home to shower. All I had been able to think about at work was Ansley and the kids. It felt like they were my family. So, I took what Jonathan was doing to them personally. He was attacking my family. Before I could get in the driveway good, my phone was ringing. "Hello?"

"Hey, Jayden. How was work?"

"It was good, Ma. How's everything?"

"It's good. I wanted to invite you and your girlfriend to dinner this coming Friday evening."

I was quiet for a moment. I didn't know if I was ready for Mama to meet her yet. Ansley was going through enough drama already. If Mama said something out of pocket to her, I would hate to have to hurt my mama's feelings. Ansley was the woman I loved, and I needed her to be able to respect that. "Jayden? You there?"

"Yes, ma'am. I was thinking, trying to remember if we had plans already. I'll mention it to Ansley."

"Okay. Well, let me know. I want to go to the grocery store by Thursday evening to get what I need."

"Okay, Mama."

"I'll let you go, sweetheart. Talk to you later. Oh, and bring the kids too."

Aww shit. Before she could hang up, I said, "You would have to be on your best behavior for me to do that."

"What do you mean by that, Jayden?"

"You know what I'm talking 'bout, Ma. No sly remarks or asking about her ex-husband in front of my babies."

"Your babies? Jayden, they aren't your children."

"Tell my heart that when Alana runs and jumps in my arms or when Sage and Garrett asks if I'm gonna be their new daddy. I love those kids like they're mine, and I need you to be able to respect that and treat them like they're mine."

"I get it, Jayden. I have step-children. You act like I'm this heartless, evil woman."

I exhaled slowly. "I know you aren't, Ma, but I'm extremely protective of them."

"I see. Well, again, call me and let me know."

"Okay."

I ended the call, then went into the house to shower. By the time I was done, I was damn near running, trying to get to Ansley and the kids. When I drove in her parents' driveway, she was sitting outside with her dad, and he was holding her in his arms. My heart sank as I stared at them. She wasn't crying, but the way she was lying in her dad's embrace, I could tell she was hurting. I slowly got out of my car and walked to the porch, trying to regulate my breathing and calm my rapidly beating heart. Ansley stood from her dad's embrace and walked to me.

I gently pulled her in my arms. "Hey, baby. You okay?

"No. Jonathan... he's trying to take my babies."

Still, there were no tears from her, but I could clearly see the sadness all over her face. "What do you mean?"

"He's taking me to court to battle for full custody."

"There's no way a judge in their right mind is going to give him full custody of the kids without proof that you are neglecting them."

"I know. I just hate going through this bullshit with him. Why won't he just let me be? He's the one that fucked up everything! Why do I feel like I've done something wrong?"

There it was. One lone tear fell down her cheek, but she quickly swiped it away. "You haven't done anything wrong, Ans. He's just a coward that doesn't want to admit he fucked up. Don't let him bring you down, baby. Where are the kids?"

"They're inside with my mother, helping her bake cookies."

Damn, this nigga was pushing hard. I was trying to contain myself for the sake of Ansley and the kids, but that shit was getting to be impossible. "Come on. Let's go inside."

I shook her dad's hand, then we walked through the door. "Jayden!" the kids yelled.

They all ran to me, giving me hugs. That only made my heart sink more. Alana held her arms up so I could pick her up. "Hey y'all. How's your day been?"

"Good," they all said.

Alana kissed my cheek. "Jayden, we baking cookies!"

"Oooh, what kind?"

"Your fav-wit!"

"How do you know what my favorite cookie is?"

"You told me you like chocolate chip! You forgot?"

I smiled brightly at her. "I sure did. I didn't think you remembered."

"I member evewything!"

"I see!"

I laughed, then spoke to Mrs. Pierre. After hugging her and stealing a cookie, causing the kids to laugh hysterically, I went to the sofa and sat next to Ansley. She was trying her best to smile with the kids, but it wasn't making it to her eyes. "Baby, what can I do?"

I grabbed her hand and kissed it, then held it between mine. "Just hold me."

"Gladly."

I wrapped my arms around her and held her close. Someone got a little jealous because she came and climbed on my lap. I kissed Alana's forehead as she laid on my shoulder. "I love y'all."

Alana lifted her head and smiled. "I love you too, Daddy."

I swallowed the lump in my throat as everyone looked at me. I didn't know what to say. Sage and Garrett walked over and sat next to us. Garrett asked, "So, you are our daddy now?"

The looks on their faces were so hopeful. No one seemed to want to tell them any differently. I finally answered. "Jonathan is your daddy. He will always be your daddy. Y'all mean everything to me, though. I love all of you, and I will be taking care of y'all too, okay?"

The three of them nodded sadly. I stood from the sofa and sat Alana where I vacated, then knelt in front of the three of them. "I'm gonna always be here for y'all."

"Daddy said that too," Sage said.

I bit my bottom lip and put my head down. Ansley knelt beside me and grabbed my hand. "Babies, listen. Your dad does want to be there for y'all. We're just having a difficult time trying to decide what's best for you."

"No, he doesn't. He's always with Belan," Garrett said.

Belan was their baby sister. Lord, these babies were having a hard time. "That's why we want Jayden to be our daddy," he added.

"Pwease Jayden?" Alana pleaded with tears in her eyes.

That caused the tears to build in my eyes. I glanced at Ansley to see her eyebrows had risen. I didn't know what to say. How could I say no to that? "Remember what I told you, Alana?"

"Yes," she said as her face brightened. "You said you would be whatever I wanted."

I nodded my head, and they all jumped on me, making me fall to the floor. I could see Mrs. Pierre staring at us with tears streaming down her face. This was going to cause a lot of confusion. I could feel it in my soul. If Jonathan came for me, I was gon' beat his fucking ass.

Finally letting me up, they ran back to the kitchen with Mrs. Pierre. I sat next to Ansley and grabbed her hand. Her face was completely red. "I'm sorry. I didn't know what else to say."

"It's okay. Neither did I. This is gonna cause more confusion though. I can feel it."

"I can feel it too."

We sat silently until Sage came with a plate of cookies and Garrett held a tall glass of milk. "Daddy, we made these for you."

My heart swelled with love for these kids, but the more it swelled, it was sinking to my feet. "Thanks, guys. I appreciate that."

"When you're done eating them, you wanna come in our room and play?"

"I sure will."

"Yay!" they both yelled.

Ansley smiled, then stole a cookie from my plate. I kissed her cheek as the boys laughed. "Do you love Mommy?" Garrett asked.

I looked Ansley in her eyes. "I sure do. Is that okay with y'all?"

They nodded their heads with huge smiles as Alana came around the corner with a plate of cookies. I watched them slide off her plate to the floor. She quickly picked them up and put them back on the plate, then walked over to us. "Here's your cookies, Mommy."

I chuckled as Ansley gave her the side-eye. She slowly took the plate from Alana. "You better eat them too, Mommy," I said with a smirk on my lips.

Ansley pushed me in the shoulder, and Alana giggled. "She's not your mommy."

"Then who is she?"

"That's your wife!"

From the mouth of babes. I glanced at Ansley, and her face was red again. "She's my girlfriend."

Alana scrunched her face as she frowned. "Why not wife?"

"We haven't gotten to that point yet. She will be my wife one day, and you can be a flower girl in our wedding."

Her eyes brightened, then she looked over at Ansley. "Really, Mommy?"

"One day, baby girl."

She hopped up and down as she giggled. God, she was the cutest little girl. As I finished my cookies, I snatched one of Ansley's and ate it too. I didn't care that it had fallen on the carpet. Mrs. Pierre's house was always clean. "My mama wants y'all to come to dinner Friday night."

"Really?"

"Yeah. She probably thinks that's the only way she'll get to see me for an extended amount of time. I blow in and blow out."

"The kids too?"

"Yep."

"If I decide to let them go with Jonathan, they won't be able to go."

She rolled her eyes just at mentioning his name. "Okay. Well, whatever the case is. Dinner is at six."

"Okay."

Once I finished, I brought my plate and glass to the kitchen and went to the room to play with my boys.

nsley

"Hello. Nice to meet you, Mrs. Jacobs."

We'd just gotten to Jayden's parents' house. His mom welcomed the kids and me inside as she looked them over like she was inspecting them. My kids were naturally shy around strangers, especially if they were in an unknown environment. So, I had to tell them to speak back to her.

Jonathan didn't have my new number yet. For all he knew, I didn't have a phone, since he had my other phone disconnected. Since he didn't try to reach out by calling my parents, I knew he didn't plan to come and get the kids. He didn't show up to even try to get them, but he wanted full custody? Yeah, right. The kids didn't seem to be phased by it. As far as they were concerned, Jayden was their daddy.

That shit had caught me by surprise. I literally did not know how to respond. Especially after they defended their reasoning for wanting Jayden to be their daddy. I knew my kids were smart for their age and probably understood more than what I gave them credit for. But their passion for wanting Jayden to be their dad still had me speechless.

Jayden introduced me to his step-dad, Allen Jacobs. He stood and hugged Alana and me, then shook the boys' hands. "So nice to finally meet y'all. You're all Jayden talks about these days."

I smiled at him, then Jayden led us to the couch. Alana sat on my lap, and the boys sat closely on either side of me. The doorbell rang before Jayden sat down, so he went to answer it. His dad glanced at us from the corner of his eye, but he didn't say anything while Jayden was gone. I thought about getting up to see if his mother needed help in the kitchen, but my babies were uncomfortable and so was I. So, I wouldn't dare leave them alone.

When Jayden came back, there was a young woman with him. She looked to be pregnant, so I assumed it was his sister. Alana frowned slightly. I playfully rolled my eyes, then whispered in her ear, "That's his sister."

Her facial expressions eased as they approached. "Hello everybody! I'm Cierra, but Jayden calls me CiCi." She grabbed Alana's hand. "You are the prettiest little girl I have ever seen. What's your name?"

"Lana," she said shyly.

"That's a pretty name."

"Thank you, CiCi."

She smiled then moved on to the boys as their mama came in the room. "Dinner is almost ready. Would anyone like anything to drink?"

"No ma'am, thank you," I responded as the kids cowered in her presence.

It was something about her that I couldn't quite put my finger on. She nodded, then returned to the kitchen. Jayden and Cierra were in conversation about how her pregnancy was going, then he turned to the boys. "Y'all wanna see my room where I slept when I was a little boy?"

They both nodded excitedly as Alana said, "Daddy, what about me?"

I closed my eyes as my breathing stopped. I could see everyone staring in shock that she'd called him daddy. No one said a word as he said, "Of course, sweetheart. Come on."

He lifted her from my lap, and they were all smiles. My phone began to ring, and I was hoping it was the doctor's office I'd interviewed at this past Tuesday. They told me they would call after hours to let me know if I had gotten the job. Unfortunately, it was Jonathan. I stood and excused myself. I didn't know how he'd gotten my number, but whatever. "Hello?"

"You didn't think it was important that I had your new number?"

"Evidently, you didn't want to communicate with me anyway. You had my phone turned off."

"It's not off. I'm just the only person that you can call from it."

I rolled my eyes. "What do you want?"

"I wanted to get the kids. I'm sorry for how I talked to you, Ansley. You're not a bitch, and I'm sorry for calling you one."

"What about having me served?"

"I still want my kids."

"Well, unfortunately, those feelings aren't mutual."

"What do you mean?"

"They said you spend all your time with Belan and don't have time for them."

"That's not true."

"Well, you can get them tomorrow. We're at Jayden's family's house for dinner."

"I don't recall you asking my permission for my kids to go there."

"I don't recall needing your permission, jackass."

"I want to get them now, Ansley."

"Jonathan, you are really testing my patience. You can either get them tomorrow morning or not at all. Take your pick."

"Ansley, dinner's ready," CiCi said from behind me.

"Okay, thank you. I'll be right there," I said to her, then went back to the call.

"I guess we'll be going to court for sure then. See you at eight in the morning."

"Fuck you, Jonathan."

I ended the call. I didn't even bother to ask how he got my number, but I was sure my mama had given it to him. He would have gotten it eventually anyway. I took a deep breath, then turned to go inside. Everyone was seated at the table as Jayden got the kids situated at the eight-chair, round table. "Sorry the call took so long," I said as I sat.

"It's okay, baby."

Jayden sat next to me. My babies looked so uncomfortable. Alana left her chair and came sat on my lap. When she did, the boys sat closer to Jayden. He looked at me as if he was trying to figure out what was wrong with the kids. He'd never witnessed them being clingy. "They are spoiled behind you, huh Ansley?" his mom asked as she brought food to the table.

"A little."

"Looks like a lot," she said under her breath, then chuckled.

I didn't respond to her comment. After sitting the roast and green beans on the table, she went back to the kitchen. Jayden stood to go help her. The moment he did, the boys sat closer to me in the chair he was previously occupying. He came back with sweet potatoes and macaroni and cheese. His mom brought out a salad and a pitcher of what looked like tea. Jayden went got glasses of ice, then they both sat. He glanced at the boys in his chair and scrunched his face up at them. They laughed.

It was strange that his dad wasn't talking to us. It was like everyone was tolerating us being there for Jayden's sake. CiCi was the only one that had been somewhat friendly, but now she was just as quiet as they were. Everyone grabbed hands, and his dad said grace. When he was done, they all dug in. Jayden fixed the boys a little of everything. "Alana can eat with me, Jayden," I said, so he wouldn't fix her a plate.

"Okay."

"So, Ansley, where do you work?" Mrs. Jacobs asked.

"Nowhere yet. I just went on an interview this past Tuesday at a doctor's office."

"Oh," she said and glanced at Jayden.

After Jayden sat a plate in front of me, I began feeding Alana. "Is your divorce final already?"

"Yes. For over four months now."

Ahh. She didn't think I was good enough for Jayden. I could sense that shit by the questions she was asking. Suddenly, my appetite was gone, and I was ready to go home. I fed Alana some mac and cheese, and she said, "Mmm. It tastes like yours, Mommy."

She smiled at Alana. Then looked at the boys as they ate their green beans. "I'm shocked they're eating those green beans. Most kids don't like vegetables."

"I've been feeding them vegetables since they were able to eat table food, so they've acquired a taste for them. They love green beans and carrots."

"That's great," CiCi said.

"Thank you."

We continued to eat as I loosened up a bit. "Lana looks just like you, Ansley. The boys must look like their dad."

"Yes, they do."

Then the dinner started to go downhill. "Is he okay with you dating Jayden?" his mom asked.

Jayden looked up from his plate with a frown on his face. "Umm, it really doesn't matter. He can't dictate anything regarding my love life."

"Well, I just didn't want to see Jayden caught up in anything if he didn't approve."

"Ma, that wasn't cool," Jayden retorted.

She rolled her eyes and stabbed a piece of roast on her plate. She continued, "So, how do you feel about Jayden?"

What kind of question was that? I guess she saw the confusion on my face, so she clarified. "Are you in love with him?"

"You know what, Gloria? That's enough."

Jayden pushed his plate away as the kids watched. "It's okay, Jay," I said as I grabbed his hand. I turned back to her. "I love Jayden. I'm not quite in love with him yet, but I know if things continue the way they are between us, it won't be long. He's my best friend, and he's a great lover."

I paused and bit my bottom lip for effect, as Jayden tried to stifle his laughter. "Jayden represents everything I want in a man. He's caring and puts us before himself all the time. He treats my kids like they're biologically his. It's why they want to call him daddy. He's shown them unconditional love, and they watch him love their mommy. He treats me like a queen, and I plan to honor him like the king he is. Forever."

Jayden squeezed my leg under the table, and I leaned over and kissed his lips. Alana giggled. "Aww, Mommy. You kissed Daddy."

I giggled with her, then kissed her forehead and fed her some green beans. The rest of dinner was silent and awkward as hell. My answer to her question shut her ass up for the night, especially when I said Jayden was a great lover. She looked like she wanted to slap the taste out of my mouth. Oh well. I didn't give a damn. I should have said he was a pro at fucking, but my kids were sitting there.

When they were done eating, Jayden asked, "Are y'all ready?"

"Ansley, you barely touched your food," CiCi said.

"I'm sorry. I don't have much of an appetite."

She smiled slightly. Alana had eaten quite a bit of it though, and the boys had cleaned their plates. "They must have been hungry," his dad said.

I was shocked that he finally said anything. "They always eat all of their food. They have big appetites."

I didn't know if he was trying to insinuate that I didn't feed my kids or what, but I was already on edge. Anybody could get it right now. I turned to Jayden. "I'm ready, babe."

"Let's go. I'm sorry about dinner. It will be a while before we come back."

I was shocked he said that shit in front of them. No one said a word, acknowledging what he said. I grabbed my kids' dishes and brought them to the kitchen, along with mine. I sat my plate on the countertop since I didn't know if she wanted the food scratched in her inside trash can or not. I followed Jayden out as Cierra walked us out.

"Jayden, why Mama acting like that?"

"I don't know but come see me before you leave. Okay?"

"Okay."

He hugged his sister, then opened my door to get in. "It was nice meeting you, Ansley. Sorry about the interrogation."

"It's okay. It was nice meeting you also."

When Jayden got in the car, he slammed the door and just sat there for a moment. "Daddy, where we going, now?"

"Y'all wanna come to my house for a little while?"

"Yay!"

I shook my head slowly. They loved Jayden's house because he had a game room. He looked at me, then grabbed my hand. "I'm so sorry, baby. That shit was so uncalled for and embarrassing as hell."

"She loves you. Her baby is too serious about a thirty-one-year-old divorcee with three children. I understand, Jay."

"I don't understand being rude, though. It's one thing to be concerned, but it's another thing to be condescending and ugly."

I didn't say anything else as we reached his house. The kids all unbuckled and got out of the Range. He came around to open my door. "They were so uncomfortable. That's why they were so quiet, huh?"

"Yes, but they are always that way when they are in an unfamiliar place and around people they don't know. They get extremely clingy and withdrawn. My mama said that I used to be that way when I was little also."

"Well, they get it honestly. Let's go inside."

"Daddy, you have some ice cream?" Sage asked.

Jayden smiled brightly, showcasing those dimples. I could tell it made him feel amazing when they called him daddy. "I sure do."

They yelled in excitement as Jayden unlocked the door. After we walked in, and we'd fixed the kids some ice cream, we sat on the sofa while they ate it. "So, Jonathan called?" Jayden asked softly.

"Yeah, he wanted to come and get them tonight. I told him that he could get them in the morning. Of course, he tried to muscle me into doing what he wanted, but that didn't happen. He's still taking me to court for custody. The call ended with me saying fuck you."

"Can I be there to meet him?"

"He's coming at eight in the morning."

"That's okay. I'll take you to breakfast afterward, and we can spend the whole day together."

"Okay. He's an idiot. I'm sure he won't act crazy with you there."

"That's why I wanna be there, baby."

I laid in his arms until the kids were done with their ice cream, then he got up to play with them in the game room. I opted to stay in the front room on the couch. Tonight had been horrible. It would be a long time before I went back to his parents' house. I hated to feel like I didn't matter. Jayden was a grown man. He didn't have kids that he had to worry about. Being with him put my sanity as well as my kids' happiness at risk.

What if this didn't work out? My kids and I would be devastated. They would feel like they'd lost two daddies. I had the most to lose. Falling for Jayden was easy, but because I was heartbroken, I made it difficult. I was scared to be hurt again, but here I was, giving us a shot. So, for her to treat me like some random floozy who was only with Jayden for what she could get out of him, hurt like hell.

Regardless of my tough exterior, I was sensitive. Just because I didn't cry or express my feelings as much, didn't mean I was emotionless. Crying was just something I tried not to do. People tended to look at tears as weakness, including myself. I never downed anyone else for crying, but it was something I tried to avoid doing at all costs ever since I stopped being a whiny little girl.

I kicked off my shoes and laid on Jayden's sofa as I listened to them have a great time together. Alana was trying to boss them. She yelled, "I the princess! Not you and not you!"

I chuckled listening to her argue with her brothers. That little girl was me made over. I tucked my feet under me and got comfortable.

ayden

I COULDN'T WAIT to meet this nigga face to face. I'd gotten to Ansley at seven-thirty and helped her finish getting the kids ready for their dad. We sat on the porch, enjoying the cool breeze as the kids rode their bicycles in the driveway. "How were they this morning when you told them their dad was coming to get them?"

"They seemed to be okay. They weren't overly excited, but they didn't seem sad either."

"Good. I hope that doesn't change when he gets here."

"I know."

Shortly after, a car turned in the driveway. We both stood, and Ansley told the kids to put their bicycles away. "Aww," Alana whined.

I could see the disappointment on their faces as Jonathan got out of the car. He had a slight frown on his face, and I did as well. In my eyes, he was less than a man for the way he was treating Ans. I grabbed the kids' overnight bags and walked toward him. The kids were walking toward him as well. He looked at me, and his expression eased up some, mine didn't.

Bitch-ass nigga. Before handing him the bags, I held my hand out and said, "Jayden."

"I'm Jonathan."

We shook hands, and both nodded, then I handed him the kids' bags. I could see the baby in the back. Ansley stood nearly behind me. "Hi, Ansley."

"Hey."

I could tell she didn't want to interact with him, and I couldn't blame her. He was trying to take the babies. "Hey daddy's baby," he said to Alana.

She glanced at me, then hugged him. That lil girl was too damned smart. He shook the boys' hands, and Sage got in the front seat. Garrett maneuvered his way between the two car seats in the back. He looked back at Alana and asked, "What's wrong, sweetheart?"

"I wanna stay with Mommy."

She started crying, and that nearly broke my heart. He hugged her tightly, but I could tell it bothered him that she didn't want to leave with him. "We're gonna have a good time, okay? I promise."

She nodded her head, and Ansley hugged her. "See you later, baby. I love you."

"I wove you too, Mommy."

"I'll bring them back Monday morning before I go to work."

Ansley nodded, her eyes never leaving Alana. Jonathan opened the back door and put Alana in her car seat. I pulled Ansley in my arms. I could tell she was worried. I was too. I was worried that he might try to keep them. If he tried to do that, it was gon' be some smoke, for real. Although I didn't play a role in creating them, they were my babies too. Taking them away from Ansley would be taking them away from me too.

After he got Alana situated and put their bags in the trunk, he shook my hand again. "Nice meeting you, Jayden. See you Monday morning, Ansley."

She only nodded again. He stared at her for a moment, then said, "I'm sorry about everything. I'm not filing for full custody, but I would like to get them as often as possible before school starts."

I could see her tension ease a bit. She took a deep breath. "Okay. Just let me know ahead of time when you want them so I won't make plans."

"Okay. Thank you."

I pulled her in my arms more as he stared for a second, then smiled tightly and got in his car. Then for some reason, what Remo said the other day popped in my mind. I bet he'd sent that dude to Ranika. I needed to call him. Jonathan was being nice because Ranika probably didn't want nothing to do with his ass anymore. Ansley hugged me tightly as we watched them drive away.

"You okay, baby?"

"Yeah. I just hate seeing them look so disappointed."

"Yeah, me too."

She moved out of my embrace, then grabbed my hand and led me inside to the room she was sleeping in. Mr. and Mrs. Pierre had left early to go work out. Ansley told me they did that three days a week. I admired their relationship, despite the bullshit that happened a few years back with Mr. Pierre and Caricia's mother. Even though Mrs. Pierre had no knowledge of the affair, I believed that even if she did, she wouldn't have left him. He did cherish her. Somehow, he'd allowed himself to get caught up with the past.

I sat on the bed as Ansley looked for something to wear. I looked her over in her t-shirt and tights. Damn, she was fine as hell, every curve made me dizzy with desire. It had been over a week since I had her, but there was no way in hell she was gonna get away from me today or tomorrow.

After pulling a pair of distressed jeans from her closet and a tank top, she turned to look at me. She held the outfit in the air for me to see. "What do you think?"

"I think that looks good. Although, it doesn't matter what you wear. You fine as hell."

She blushed as I stood and walked closer to her. Her breathing seemed to have stopped as she stared up at me. I pulled her hips into mine, and she dropped the clothes on the floor. Pulling my face to hers, she kissed me passionately. As I moaned into her mouth, I lowered my hands and gripped her ass. I slid my tongue in her mouth as we groped each other.

Slowly breaking our kiss, I backed away from her. The flames danced in her eyes as her chest rose and fell. Those nipples were begging to be teased, and I was just the man for the job. That was until I heard car doors closing. Ansley poked her lip out, as I smiled. I bit my bottom lip, then made my way to the front room and sat on the sofa. "Hey, Jayden," Mrs. Pierre said.

"Hey. How are y'all?"

"Tired as hell," Mr. Pierre said, then laughed. "Thelma, I'm going take a shower."

"Okay, honey." She went to the kitchen and washed her hands. "So, what are you and Ansley up to today?"

"We're going to breakfast when she gets done getting dressed. I don't know what we'll do after that."

Shiiiiid. I knew exactly what the hell we would be doing. Ain't no way I was about to tell her mama that shit though. Just thinking about how my mama's face had screwed up when Ansley said I was a good lover had me smiling. She didn't ask shit else after that. "Well, that's nice. I hope you and Ansley have a great time. She's been so stressed."

"Yeah. Hopefully, I can get her out of this funk she's in. Alana cried when it was time to leave with her daddy."

"Ooh, my poor baby. I know that almost killed Ansley."

"Why doesn't she cry much? She's been in a lot of pain over this break up with Jonathan, but I've only seen her cry a couple of times. Even then, she hurries to compose herself."

Mrs. Pierre sat next to me. "I think it's somewhat my fault that she holds her emotions in a lot. When she was little, she used to whine a whole lot. I would fuss at her and tell her she was being a baby. Only babies whined like that. By the time she turned seven, she was barely crying anymore."

"She took it to the extreme."

"Yeah, she did. Her dad and I got in the biggest argument about it. I sat her down and explained that I didn't mean she shouldn't cry when she was hurt. I just didn't want her crying when we'd said no to something she wanted or when she couldn't get her way. It didn't help though."

I nodded in understanding. Ansley was stubborn at times, so I could only imagine. Her mama took a deep breath and shook her head slowly. "She's so stubborn. Since day one. Didn't want to cry when the doctor slapped her bottom."

I chuckled as Ansley walked up front, looking sexy as hell. "What's so funny? What are y'all talking about?"

"You. Are you ready?"

"After I hear about what y'all said about me."

Her mom and I laughed at her stubbornness. "Just that you're stubborn. You've proven our point," Mrs. Pierre said.

Ansley rolled her eyes. "I'm ready, Jayden."

I led her outside to my Range and held the door open for her. Once I'd gotten inside, I handed her an envelope. "What's this?"

"Just open it, baby."

She opened it, and her lips parted slightly. So damn sexy. "You paid for me a spa day?"

"Yeah. I know you've been stressed. I just wanted to give you something that you would enjoy and help you destress, other than me."

She giggled. "Thank you, Jay. Although, you're enough."

"Keep on, and we gon' skip breakfast."

"No, we won't."

She leaned over and rubbed her hand over my erection. I know like hell she wasn't about to do what I thought she was gon' do. Ansley looked in my eyes, and I saw that raw passion plain as day.

She unzipped my jeans, then freed him and licked her lips. *Shit!* She had my shit leaking already. "Jay, damn, I love your dick." As she stroked him a couple of times, her eyes met mine. "I love you too."

Before I could respond and ask if she was saying what I thought, she leaned over and pulled him in her mouth. Her mouth felt so damned good. I couldn't believe she was sucking my dick while I was driving and in broad daylight. This was some damned Roc and Shay shit for real. Feeling her spit roll to my balls, caused me to moan loudly in response. "Fuck, Ans. Shit."

She hummed and continued to deep-throat my shit while I drove. It was killing me not to close my eyes and lay my head back. Her hand wrapped around the base of my dick as I felt her gag on it. I grabbed a handful of her hair as she bobbed on it. "I'm 'bout to bust, Ans."

We stopped at the red light, so I glanced from right to left. I broke out in a sweat as a dump truck stopped next to us. "Ans, I'm sure he can see everything you're doing."

She released her suction. "So what. Let him watch."

Now, that shit, literally made me bust. "Fuck, girl!" The light changed, so I took off as she swallowed my shit. "Your ass in trouble after breakfast."

She sat up, and I noticed some of my nut on her lips. "You got some on them DSL's, Ans."

She gave me a slight smile, then she licked them seductively. "Did I get it all?"

"Uh huh," I said, barely being able to tear my gaze away from her.

She had a nigga sprung. As we parked in a spot at Golden Corral, she looked in the mirror and fixed her hair, then touched up her lipstick. I stared at those beautiful, purple lips that were wrapped around my dick a minute ago. "Ans, damn. That shit was so good. Don't go in there and get all full. I ain't gon' be able to wait after this."

She giggled as I got out to open her door. When I did, her phone rang. She answered on speaker. "Hello?"

"You mind telling me why the fuck my kids calling him daddy?"

She exhaled and let her head drop back. "They see him more than they see you, Jonathan. So, ask yourself that damn question. He told them that you are their father, but they said you don't spend time with them. So, unlike that bitch Ranika, Jayden didn't tell them to call him daddy. He was actually against it, but the kids insisted."

"I don't believe that shit. My kids love me."

"Why don't you take the time to sit them down and talk to them. They'll tell you, just like they tell me all the bullshit you do."

"Yeah. Whatever. You need to rectify this shit, immediately, or I'm gon' make your fucking life miserable."

"I doubt that, nigga," I said, coming to Ansley's defense.

He was quiet for a minute, then said, "No disrespect, bruh, but this shit between me and Ansley."

"Naw, sound like you got a problem with me, and I ain't yo' fuckin' bruh. You gon' come at her better than that, or you gon' have to see me. Don't let my size fool you. You don't want this."

Ansley was staring at me with her mouth open. She'd never heard me go there with nobody. I didn't like confrontation, but I wasn't gon' let nobody disrespect my woman or me. "Whatever. All I know is that my kids ain't gon' be calling nobody else daddy. Point, blank, period."

"Jonathan, again, if you were doing what you should be doing, you wouldn't have to worry about that. Now quit fucking harassing me."

"You ain't seen harassment. I haven't called my attorney yet to say we weren't going to court, but you best believe, we going now."

"I can't stand yo' fucking ass. I hate you, Jonathan. You hear that shit? I hate you!"

She ended the call and dropped her phone in her purse. I pulled her in my arms as I tried to calm my own nerves. I was angry as hell. Ansley lifted her head from my chest. "Why he keep fucking with me?"

Her heart was beating rapidly against my ribcage, and her face was red as hell. "Don't worry, baby. I got his ass."

"I told you before, Jayden, that I don't want you involved in this shit. You hear me? I don't want you in this shit!"

She pushed away from me and folded her arms across her chest. "What the hell you want me to do, Ans? Let him keep disrespecting you and holding the kids as pawns for you to do what he wants? That's bullshit, and you know it!"

"No, it isn't. This is my drama, my business. Let me handle it!"

"It *is* bullshit! So, you want me to be a pussy-ass nigga, and just let him talk to you however he wants, right?"

"Jayden, just take me home."

"You can't be fucking serious right now."

"Yes, I'm fucking serious. Bring me home."

I was so angry, I walked away from her and got in the Range and waited on her to get in. Just because I had a great personality and was playful most of the times, she expected me to be passive and a hoe-ass nigga. That wasn't gon' happen. She got in and put her face in her hands. "Look. I love you with my life. Why you don't want me to defend you?"

"Because I don't need representation. I can defend my fucking self. I asked you to stay out of it."

"Then you shouldn't have answered the damn phone on speaker."

"That shit don't matter now."

"What the fuck that's supposed to mean?"

"That your mama was right. We don't need to be together."

"See... you know what? Cool. I'm gon' bring you home."

My heart was crushed. There was no denying that. I drove back to her parents' house with a frown on my face. When I got there, she jumped out without saying a word. I watched her walk to the back door as my heart tried to harden. Just the effort of that was causing my face to twitch. I backed out of the driveway and peeled out without taking another look.

13

nsley

I WALKED through the back door and went straight to my room as my parents stared at me. Why couldn't Jayden let me handle this myself? Him getting involved was only gonna make the shit worse. Why couldn't he see that? My phone started ringing again. "Hello?"

My baby was crying in the background. I sat straight up in the bed. "Am I on speaker, again? Yo' dude don't know how to mind his business."

I rolled my eyes. "What's wrong with Alana?"

"She wants to go meet you. I sat them down and told them they were not to call that nigga daddy. I'm their daddy. Then she started crying behind that nigga and wants to go home."

"Jonathan! She's three years old. I'm coming to get my babies. You a fucking asshole."

"You will not come to get them. She gon' get over it. I told her to hush her mouth. I'm getting sick of all that crying."

I put my head down and recalled those same words from my youth. Only, this situation was different. I was in a loving home. Alana and the boys weren't feeling any love from their father, which was why they were so quick to call Jayden daddy. *Jayden.* I fought the lump in my throat. "I'm on my way, Jonathan. Let me talk to them."

He ended the call. I grabbed my purse and left the room. "What's going on, princess?"

"The usual," I responded on my way out the door.

I didn't give them time to ask any more questions. Getting in my Traverse, I put my head on the steering wheel trying to calm my nerves. Jonathan was really trying to take me there. I had to be calm for my babies. It would only make the situation worse if I was hysterical. Then they would definitely want to leave with me.

I knocked on the back door, and Jonathan opened it almost immediately. "She's fine now, Ansley. Seeing you is only going to make her cry again."

"Then I'll stay until she goes down for her nap."

He stepped aside and let me in. When Alana saw me, she ran to me. "Mommy!"

The boys came running to me also. Belan was on the floor on her blanket watching them. "What's going on, y'all?"

"Daddy said we couldn't call Jayden daddy."

I looked up at him and decided to tell our kids the truth. "Jayden is okay with you guys calling him Jayden. Your dad is just insecure. He knows he hasn't been the best dad that he could be, lately, and he feels like Jayden is taking his place."

"Ansley..."

"Is that not the truth, Jonathan?"

The kids all looked at him, so he remained quiet. "So, for now, just call him Jayden like you used to, okay?"

The boys nodded but, Alana wasn't feeling that at all. "I call him daddy!"

"Baby, please just call him Jayden, so you won't hurt your dad's feelings and his ego."

"Kids go to your rooms. Your mom and I need to talk."

The boys went to their room, but Alana was hugging me tightly. "Alana, you too."

"But I want Mommy."

"Go to your room, sweetheart. It's okay."

She loosened her grip, and I sat on the couch. When she went to her room, Jonathan sat next to me. "I can't believe you said that to our kids."

"Jonathan, it's the truth. I always knew I would be the kind of mother that wouldn't hide things from her kids. They deserve the truth."

"That wasn't truth though. I don't feel threatened by his presence."

"Okay. Whatever."

I didn't want to talk about Jayden. Thinking about the way I yelled at him, was making my heart heavy. I sat back on the sofa, and so did Jonathan. Putting my hands over my face, I exhaled loudly. When I removed them, Jonathan's lips landed on mine. For a moment, I got caught up. I guess because of the familiarity of them. The moment my mind registered what was happening, I jumped back away from him.

"What are you doing?"

"I just couldn't resist those pouty lips any longer. I'm sorry."

I wiped my mouth, then scooted away from him. *Jayden.* My heart longed for him, but I couldn't continue to bring him down. Alana came back to the front room. "Mommy okay?"

"I'm okay, baby," I said, holding my arms out to her.

She didn't seem convinced, but I didn't sound very convincing either. Jonathan sat back and watched me hold Alana. "I'm surprised he didn't come with you."

I looked at him and mouthed the words *fuck you.* Wanting to cry was a feeling I always had, but from years of practice, I still suppressed the feeling. Breaking it off with Jayden was eating away at my insides. I silently rocked my baby, until she had gone to sleep.

After taking her to her room and laying her in the bed, I turned to leave the room and ran right into Jonathan. He held me to keep me from falling to the floor until I got my balance.

We walked out of her room, and I grabbed my purse from the sofa. Before I could walk away, Jonathan gently grabbed my arm. When I turned to look at him, he pulled me closer. "Jonathan, what?"

"I know it doesn't seem like it, but I still love you, Ans. Seeing you move on is making me crazy."

"Why? You moved on while we were still married."

He dropped his head, took a deep breath, then looked back up at me. "I'm sorry. I just wish we could try again, but I can tell he loves you. Do you love him?"

"It doesn't matter."

"Did he break up with you?"

"No. I broke up with him. Now if you're done ruining my life, I'm going back to my parents' house."

He let me go as I swallowed the lump in my throat. I walked away with my head hanging. My chest and head were hurting. It was best to let Jayden go so he wouldn't try to be so involved in my drama. When I got to the car, my cell phone was ringing. "Hello?"

"Hello. Ms. Malveaux?"

"Yes?"

"I'm calling from Dr. Sprout's office. I was calling to tell you that we would like to offer you the position. When can you start?"

"I can start Monday. Thank you so much."

"Yes, ma'am. Enjoy your weekend."

I ended the call. I wasn't expecting them to call me on a Saturday. The first person I wanted to call was Jayden. *Jayden.* Depression was looming over me like a rain cloud. Starting the engine, I put the car in gear and headed back home. When I got there, Remo's truck was there. *Great.* I hoped he hadn't talked to Jayden. *Jayden.* It seemed whenever I thought about him, my heart was echoing the sentiments.

Whether I wanted to accept it or not, my heart needed him. It hadn't been a whole two hours since I left him, but to my heart, it felt like an eternity. I walked in the house to see Remo talking to Mama. "Hey, Ans. Where's Jayden? I've been trying to call him since nine this morning, and he won't answer his phone."

I ignored him and walked straight to my room. I heard him say, "Aww, hell."

I closed the door, but I was sure Remo would be entering soon. As I figured, before I could sit on the bed, he'd walked in. "Ans, what's going on?"

I was doing my best not to cry. Talking about it would make me cry. Although I knew I could be vulnerable around Remo, I just didn't want to. "We broke up."

"What? Why?"

"I don't want to talk about it, Remo."

"This got to do with Jonathan, doesn't it? I know you not going back to that fucker."

"No, I'm not."

"I need to whoop his ass one good time. When is he bringing the kids back?"

"Remo! Please, just leave. I need to be alone. Okay?"

I was begging him. The tears were starting to fill my eyes, but there was no way I was gonna let them drop, especially not in front of him. It was bad enough Jayden had seen me break a few times. He nodded his head, then left the room. I laid in the bed on my side. *Jayden.* My heart wanted to communicate with his. It wanted to say, *I'm sorry, Jay.*

––––––––

"Ansley, this is Nakia. She'll be training you to use our software," Dr. Sprout said.

"Nice to meet you, Nakia."

"Likewise," she said, shaking my hand.

She seemed to have a slight attitude. Hopefully, that disappeared once she started training me. The doctor introduced me to more women around the office, but I was barely paying attention. The past couple of days, my heart had been screaming for Jayden. I stayed in the room the rest of the day Saturday and all day Sunday. Jonathan had dropped the kids off this morning and gave me a single rose to congratulate me on my new job.

My eyes were somewhat puffy since I hadn't been getting much sleep. Trying to detox my body of Jayden had proven to be more difficult than I thought it would be. He called yesterday, but I couldn't answer. Although, my heart was about to beat out of my chest when I saw his name on the caller ID. My body longed for him too. He was supposed to punish me Saturday morning, and all that went to hell in a hand-basket.

After all the introductions, I went to my desk and put my pictures up of the kids as I waited for Nakia. I'd been home with them for almost nine months. So, to say I missed them terribly was an understatement. Just as I was about to text my mom, Nakia said, "Okay, Ms. Ansley. Let's get started. Have they given you a user name and password yet?"

"Yes, ma'am."

"Okay. Go ahead and key it in."

I did as she said, then waited for further instruction. She'd stopped to answer the phone. Again, I stared at pictures of the kids with my chin propped up on my hand. "Ooh, you have twins. And this little diva is adorable."

I smiled. "Thank you."

"How old are they?"

"My twins, Sage and Garrett are six, and Alana is three."

"How precious. I'm sorry. They're so cute, they distracted me for a moment."

I giggled. She began showing me the new system that was extremely easy to learn. By lunchtime, I was processing insurance payments by myself with little assistance. My phone had been vibrating all morning with calls from Jonathan. He was getting on my fucking nerves. I grabbed my purse to go eat the lunch I brought from home in the car.

As I stepped out and got to the elevator, I was so engrossed in what I was looking at on my phone, I walked right into a man getting off the elevator. "Oh my God. I'm so sorry."

When I looked up, I was met with a gorgeous pair of hazel eyes. He had on a white coat, so I was assuming he was a doctor. "It's okay. You okay?"

"Yes, thank you."

"Alright."

He walked away, but not before staring into my eyes. Goodness, he was beautiful. I walked on the elevator, and as I turned around, I saw him standing there watching me from the hallway. Okay, that was a little on the creepy side now. As I got to my car, my phone was vibrating again. *Shit!* "Jonathan what? It's my first day."

"Ranika and Belan got in a car accident."

"What?"

"Ranika is dead, and my baby is in ICU," he cried. "They were hit by a car that they are assuming possibly ran a red light."

"Oh my God, Jonathan. I'm so sorry."

Regardless of who they were, Belan was an innocent baby. She wasn't a year old yet. "Would you and the kids come to be with me when you get off?"

"Of course. I'll come over when I get off. Damn, I'm so sorry. What hospital?"

"Thanks, Ans. Hermann Memorial, Baptist."

"Okay. See you later."

"Okay."

Damn, I couldn't believe this shit. As much as I couldn't stand Ranika, I would have never wanted her to die. Even though I may have visualized myself killing her. But that baby. Lord. I felt a heaviness in my heart for Jonathan. I could never imagine what it was like to almost lose a child. That would kill me to see one of my babies that way.

I ate my sandwich, then went back to my desk. Staring at my babies had me in my feelings a bit, so I was extremely quiet for the rest of the day.

ayden

IF SHE WASN'T DYING by now, then she wasn't for me to begin with. It had been two days, and I hadn't heard from Ansley. I tried calling yesterday after I cooled off, but she didn't answer. When I got off work, Remo was sitting in my driveway. He was off today so he couldn't run me down at work. He'd been calling me since Saturday, but I hadn't answered or returned his calls. I was almost sure that he had an idea of what was going on by now.

I parked in my garage, then met him outside. "Man, what in the hell is going on? Ansley said y'all broke up."

"She didn't tell you why?"

"No, she said she didn't want to talk about it. I been tryna hunt yo' ass down since Saturday when I left her at Mama and Daddy's house."

I unlocked the door, and we went inside and sat at the wet bar.

"She broke up with me because she wanted me to let Jonathan say whatever the fuck he wanted to say without getting at him. She doesn't want me involved in her drama."

"What the fuck?"

"That was my response. He was hollering at her over the phone, and she had that shit on speaker. What kind of man would I be to let that shit go down without putting him in his place? I told her I wasn't the pussy-ass nigga she wanted me to be."

"That's bullshit. I told her a long time ago that she needed to be fucking done with Jonathan before she pursued anything with you."

"She ain't gon' ever be completely done with him as long as they have kids together. Lana is only three."

"What was he tripping about?"

"The kids started calling me daddy."

"Oh, wow."

"Yeah. As much as we tried to discourage them from doing so, they insisted. Who can say no to Alana's little voice saying, pwease?"

"No damn body. Ansley tripping, for real. I'm sorry, Jay. I know you hurting. You ain't gotta tell me."

"Man, I ain't ate since Saturday."

"Nigga, you more than hurt if you can't eat."

"She won't answer my calls either."

"She so fucking stubborn. Maybe I can get Caricia to talk to her. It's a little harder now since she's working."

"I ordered flowers to be delivered to Dr. Sprout's office for her Wednesday."

"So, you aren't giving up?"

"No. I love her, Remo. Giving up isn't an option."

"I'm gonna be honest with you, Jayden. I love my sister, but I need you to be prepared if she doesn't come around. Protect your heart. Again, Ansley is extremely stubborn."

As if I didn't feel bad enough. "Man, you don't feel what I feel when we're together. I know she feels it too."

He lifted his hands in surrender. "I'm just saying. I know Ansley, and I know you too."

Who knew her better than Remo? Maybe I should take his advice. I dropped my head and almost shed a tear. Ansley and those kids were my world. "Maybe you're right."

He laid his hand on my back. "In the meantime, I'm still gonna get Caricia to talk to her. I may even try to talk to her again myself."

"Don't worry about it, Remo. If she wants to talk to me, she will, without persuasion."

He nodded, then we both went to the living room and sat on the couch. I laid my head back as Remo turned the TV on. "Where's Caricia?"

"She went to dinner with her mama. You know other than you, that's her best friend."

"Yeah, I know."

"Well, go shower and get dressed. You need to eat, and I'm not taking no for an answer."

I stood from the sofa and left him sitting there without a word. When I got to the bathroom and started the shower, I sent Ansley a text.

I've been thinking about you a lot. I miss you, Ansley. Please think about your decision. I can't see myself living without you and the kids. Loving you and being with you has been like a dream come true. I love you so much, and it's killing me not to talk to you. See you. Touch you. Kiss those beautiful lips. You are the only woman I want to do those things with. Please text or call me.

I got in the shower and hoped I would have a response when I got out.

———

"You like Charlie's Barbeque, right?"

"Yeah, that's fine."

Remo and I were going to get something to eat. Ansley had never messaged me back, and I was starting to think that Remo was right. When we got to Charlie's, I saw a Traverse that looked like hers. My eyes met Remo's, then I hurriedly got out of the car. Practically running inside, I came to screeching halt, when I saw her standing there with Jonathan and the kids. His arm was loosely wrapped around her waist, and she seemed comfortable with it. "Jayden!" Alana screamed.

It took everything in me not to run right out the door. I smiled tightly at her, then looked up at Ansley. I nodded at her, then shook the boys' hands and hugged Alana. Remo came in and stopped in his tracks, just as I had done. Ansley looked like she wanted to say something, but before she could, I turned and walked out the door.

Remo unlocked the car , and I got in. Taking deep breaths was becoming more difficult. I felt like I was about to blow a gasket. The only thing I could do was bend over and rest my head on the dash. This shit was unreal. She'd gone back to him after all that shit? It was like our time together meant nothing to her. I sat up and put my seatbelt on, waiting on Remo to come out. She didn't even have the decency to try to come after me.

She owed me an explanation. It felt like she had my heart in her hands and was ringing that shit out like it was a wet towel. Finally, Remo came out and got in the car with a frown on his face. I didn't ask any questions. As we rode in silence, I replayed the scene in my head. The kids called me Jayden again. I wondered what they were told for that to happen.

Remo went through the drive-thru at Popeyes and ordered some chicken while I sulked, like a sick puppy. *Man up, Jayden, and quit acting like a bitch.* I sat up in my seat and grabbed the chicken from Remo. That damn smell had my stomach growling. Loudly. "Well damn. I guess you back."

I forced a chuckle as he glanced at me. We went back to my house and dug into our chicken, red beans and rice, and biscuits while watching a pre-season football game. Remo kept glancing at me, but once he noticed that I caught those glances, he decided to say what was on his mind. "That was some hurtful shit. You wanna talk about it?"

"Naw, not really."

"Okay."

We continued eating and watching the game in silence.

————

IT HAD BEEN a week since that dreadful day I saw Ansley at Charlie's. She had yet to try to call me or respond to my text message, which led me to believe that Remo was right. I was trying to move on, but that had been so difficult. Thoughts of her flooded my mind daily. That was only causing me to be more depressed, regardless of how hard I was trying to fight it.

Walking through the grocery store, I noticed this chick that kept staring at me. She seemed to always be in the vicinity, no matter where I went. Usually, I liked to be the one to show interest first, but with my mind being preoccupied with Ansley, that would be impossible right now. The last time our eyes met, I held her gaze and smiled. She smiled back and walked closer. As I threw a bag of corn on the cob in my buggy, she said, "You have gorgeous dimples."

I smiled again. "Thank you. I'm Jayden."

I held my hand out for hers, and she placed it in mine. "I'm Korliss."

"Nice to meet you. I like your name."

"Thank you. It's nice to meet you also. Are you from this area?"

"Yes. I've been in Beaumont all my life. What about you?"

"I came here to attend Lamar. I'm originally from Huntsville, but I have family here."

"That's cool. You still in school?"

"No. I graduated almost two years ago."

"So, you're about twenty-four?"

"Exactly. How old are you?"

"Twenty-five. What did you go to school for?"

"I'm a teacher."

"That's cool. My best friend is a teacher. She graduated almost two years ago too."

"What's her name?"

"Caricia Edwards."

"I don't think I know her. So, what do you do?"

"I'm a process operator at ExxonMobil."

We continued talking as we walked around the store, occasionally dropping items in our baskets. Once we'd checked out and had made it outside, I decided to make a move. "So, can I have your number, Korliss?"

"I thought you'd never ask."

I smiled at her, then dialed her number in my phone and called her, so she could have my number as well. "I'll try to call you tonight if you aren't going to be busy."

"I'll be at home. I can't wait to talk to you more, Jayden."

"Likewise."

I grabbed her hand and sadly, I felt nothing. It wasn't like the first time I touched Ansley. I let her hand go and walked away, feeling my shoulders slump a little. Once I loaded the groceries in my Range, I glanced over at Korliss getting in her Camaro. She was cute, but she wasn't Ansley. She was short, barely to my shoulder and medium brown skinned. She had big hair and a beautiful smile... but she wasn't Ansley.

After getting in, I headed home to do nothing. I was off today and would be off for the next two days as well. Remo would be off Sunday, so maybe we would kick it then. I carried the groceries in the house, then put on some corn on the cob. I was making a grilled chicken salad with corn on the cob and Sister Schubert dinner rolls. I turned on the oven, then put the rest of the groceries away.

Tomorrow, I'd probably drive out to Houston to see my sister. I needed to get away from this house. I hadn't talked to my mama in a few days, which was crazy too. Usually, I talked to my mama almost every day. So, to go almost a week and not hear her voice was weighing on me as well. She'd called to apologize for her behavior, but Ansley and I had broken up already. I didn't bother telling her, because I couldn't bear to hear her say I told you so.

She probably wouldn't say those exact words, but she would use the situation to justify her behavior. She'd say something like, *I was trying to protect you from this very thing.* I needed Ansley. Grabbing my phone, I decided to call her. Being sprung wasn't fun. It felt like Ansley had snatched my fucking manhood from me. "He-wo?"

I swallowed the lump in my throat. Alana must have been playing on Ansley's phone. "Hey, lil mama."

"Jayden! We miss you! Where are you?"

"I'm at home. I miss y'all too."

"Mommy looks sad."

"Why?

"She fussed at daddy."

"Oh. Are y'all moving back with him?"

"No, silly. We at Grandma and Grandpa house."

"Give me that phone, Alana. Who are you talking to?"

Just hearing her voice had the tear falling down my cheek. The phone went silent, and I thought Alana had ended the call until I heard Ansley say, "Boys, go take your bath."

Shortly after, the call ended. I tried calling back, but the phone only rang.

nsley

I THINK I was falling into a depression. Miserable was only lightly describing how I felt. Jonathan's baby was still in ICU, and the doctors were recommending that he take her off life support. He'd adamantly refused. Jonathan was falling apart more and more every day as he watched his daughter clinging to life. I'd been bringing the kids up there daily.

When I saw Jayden at Charlie's, it felt like I was stuck in wet cement and someone had superglued my tongue to the roof of my mouth. Seeing the hurt on him crushed me. I knew me being there with Jonathan didn't look good. It didn't help that Jonathan was so affectionate toward me. I'd let him get away with it because I knew he was having a hard time. Clearly, Jayden saw it as more.

I was so embarrassed, I could barely look at him. I'd cut him deep, and it only made me hurt that much more. Being with him was a bad decision. I'd brought him into my drama, then expected him to be able to ignore it. That was wrong of me to even ask him to do such a thing.

I took the phone from Alana. "Alana, go in the room."

I'd heard her talking to someone, so I accessed my call logs. *Jayden.* She was talking to him, and now he was calling back. God, I couldn't. But I missed him so much. It stopped ringing, but I decided I needed to talk to him about what he saw. After turning the TV off, I checked on the boys to find them full of suds. I closed the door, then checked to see Alana in bed under the covers. She smiled at me. "Mommy? I talked to Jayden."

"I see."

"I told him Mommy sad."

I lowered my head. If my babies knew I was sad, then I needed to do something about it. The boys came in the room to kiss Alana and me goodnight and say their prayers. Once they were done, they went to their room. Alana snuggled against me. "Mommy?"

"Yes, baby?"

"You call Jayden?"

"Yeah, I'm gonna call him."

This little girl was like my best friend. She was so mature for her age and seemed to understand things that she shouldn't. I dialed his number, and he answered on the first ring. "Hello?"

I closed my eyes tightly. "Hi, Jayden."

"Damn, Ans. I miss you."

He sounded like he was crying, and my heart felt like it was breaking in two. "I needed to explain."

"Okay," he said softly.

"Jonathan's daughter, Belan, and her mother were in a bad car wreck. Ranika died, but Belan is in ICU at Baptist. We'd left from there to get something to eat."

Charlie's Barbeque was right across the street from the hospital so Jayden would know that it wasn't a friendly outing. "So, you and Jonathan aren't back together?"

"No. He was in his feelings since his little girl is barely clinging to life. They're trying to convince him to let go. I allowed him to put his arm around me, and I shouldn't have. I was just feeling sorry for him, that's all. I'm so sorry for not explaining it then, but I was frozen in place at the sight of you."

"Thank you for that explanation. I thought you didn't care about me."

"Jayden, I could never stop caring about you. I'm sorry it seemed like I didn't. I thought you were beyond pissed at me."

"I was. It wore off, though. Now, I just miss you."

"Okay, well I have to go. Alana isn't going to go to sleep until I stop talking."

"Can I talk to her for a second?"

"Yeah."

I handed the phone to Alana, and she sat up with a smile on her face. "Hi, Jayden... I miss you too... Mommy misses you too..." I rolled my eyes, and she giggled. "I love you too. When you come to Grandma and Grandpa house? We want to see you... Sage hit me... Garrett hit Sage, and said don't do that, Sage!"

"Okay Alana, that's enough."

"Mommy say that's enough. Bye Jayden."

"Hello?"

"Ansley, I love you, and I want you in my life. I know you don't want me in yours, but I can't let go."

"I'm sorry, Jayden. I have too much drama."

"Stop letting Jonathan control you. I'm waiting, but I can't wait forever, Ans. I love you." I couldn't respond. My nerves were all over the place. "Goodnight, Ans."

"Goodnight, Jayden."

I ended the call, and Alana kissed my cheek. "Mommy miss Jayden."

"Yeah."

She rubbed my cheek, and the tear I had in a choke hold fell to the pillow. Thankfully it was the side I was laying on, so Alana didn't see it. Just as we were both dozing, my phone was ringing. "Hello?"

"She's gone, Ansley."

"Oh no. I'm so sorry, Jonathan. Did you stop the life support?"

"No. She died while she was on it. The funeral home just left with her."

"God, I'm so sorry."

"Can I get the kids tomorrow?"

"Yeah, I'll bring them over."

"Thank you, Ans. I'll call you tomorrow."

"Okay."

————

I DREAMED about Jayden all night. Something would happen in the dream that would cause me to wake up, then I'd go back to sleep and pick up where I left off. I was so glad today was Saturday, and I didn't have to work. Nap time would be for me too. It was eight, and it felt like I'd only gotten two hours of sleep. After getting up and brushing my teeth and Alana's, I went to the kitchen to fix her some cereal.

"Thank you, Mommy."

"You're welcome, sweetheart."

As I started my coffee, there was a knock at the back door. My heart sped up, and my temperature rose. My parents didn't have visitors. Remo and Caricia came over often, but they rarely knocked. My hair was all over the place. I tightened my short, silk robe and went to the door. I looked out the blinds, and I rested my head on the glass. It was Jayden.

"Ans, please open the door."

I swallowed the lump in my throat and opened it. He stood there looking sexy as ever in his black and gray t-shirt and gray jogging pants. He looked sexy in whatever he wore. After staring at me as my chest rose and fell, he made his way in the house and immediately wrapped me in his arms. "Jayden!"

Alana almost knocked over her cereal trying to get to him. He scooped her up in his arms and hugged her tightly. Then I saw the tear fall from his eye. *God, help me.* "Jayden, I missed you." Alana put her head down and continued. "Daddy said I can't call you daddy, Jayden."

I swallowed hard as Jayden glanced at me, then looked in her eyes. "That's okay. It doesn't change our relationship. We will still be close whether you call me daddy, Jayden, or Mr. Incredible."

She giggled and hugged his neck as I smiled, putting my hand to my chest. He put her down, and she ran back to her cereal. When my eyes met his, it felt like they were pulling me to him. It was at that moment that I decided to stop fighting what I was feeling. I was in love with him. The issues between me and Jonathan weren't worth losing him over. He didn't deserve the drama, but neither did I. As I was about to make my way to him, his phone rang.

He looked at the caller ID, then back at me. Deciding to answer the call, he said, "Hello?... Hi Korliss... I'm okay and you?"

The courage I'd just filled up inside of me like a helium filled balloon, was deflating quickly. He was talking to someone else. I could feel my heart breaking. As I was about to walk off to sit next to Alana, I heard him say, "Well, I am in love with someone. We're trying to work through our difficulties. When I met you, I thought we were done."

My eyebrows had risen slightly, and I looked back at him. He continued, "Okay... Enjoy your weekend."

Putting my apprehensiveness and pride aside, I ran to him and fell in his arms. For the first time in a long time, I let my emotions free. My body rocked as he held me tightly and rubbed my head. I could hear Alana whimper. "Mommy okay?"

I broke away from Jayden and saw she was standing next to us. Stooping, I pulled her in my arms. "Mommy's okay. I'm just happy."

I wiped her tears away as the boys came in the kitchen. When they saw Jayden, they ran to him. Watching my kids with him, made me feel extremely guilty. I had been selfish. Jayden was so important to them, and I'd pushed him out of their lives for my own selfish agenda. Instead of helping the situation, what I convinced myself I was doing, I'd hurt the four most important people in my life.

After hugging the boys, Jayden pulled me back in his arms and kissed my lips. Damn, I missed him. "Ooooh, Jayden kiss Mommy!"

I rolled my eyes at Alana's dramatics. He smiled, then said in my ear, "I love you."

"I love you too, Jay. I'm in love with you. Forgive me for hurting you. I was so selfish."

"It's okay, baby. Are you really in love with me?"

I swiped the tears away that continued to fall. "Yes, and my heart feels whole again, now that you're here. I don't want to lose you again."

He held me tightly against him. *God, this feels so much better.* Situations can cause you to make decisions that you think are right for everyone involved. While I thought I was shielding him from the drama in my life, I was giving Jonathan a free pass to dictate how I lived my life. Now that I'd come to that realization, life felt so much easier.

"You never lost me, Ans. Just don't push me away. I love you too much for that. The past two weeks have been hard as hell."

"For me too."

He let me go so I could fix the boys cereal, then he followed Alana and me to our room. "What's on your agenda today?"

"I'm bringing the kids to meet their dad." I glanced down at Alana. I hadn't told the kids yet. I looked back at him and mouthed, *she died.*

I saw Jayden's eyes sadden. Everyone's heart turned to mush when they heard that a baby had died. "Can I ride with you?"

"Of course."

I helped Alana get dressed and packed her an overnight bag. Jonathan needed their company. I could only imagine the depression he was feeling in that house all alone. Ranika's funeral was last weekend. Now he would have to plan a funeral for his baby. Belan was barely seven months old. I proceeded to comb Alana's hair as Jayden watched.

Once the boys joined us in the room in jean shorts and t-shirts, I sat them all down on the bed. "Listen. I need to tell y'all something." Their eyes were big, and they had smiles on their faces. Only, I knew what I was about to say was gonna wipe the smiles right off. "You guys know that Belan was really sick."

"Yes, ma'am. I hope she gets better," Sage said.

I put my head down for a moment as Jayden held my hand. "Belan died last night. I'm so sorry that you don't have your baby sister anymore."

I watched their smiles turn upside down, and they all started crying. "She's gonna be an angel now. Your dad is really sad, and he needs you guys to keep him company. You think y'all can do that?"

"Yes ma'am," the boys said.

"So, we can't play with Belan no more?" Alana asked.

I wiped her tears from her eyes. "No baby. God thought she was better as an angel. She will be looking at you from above, protecting you. Okay?"

"Potec'ing me from what?"

"Whatever tries to come your way to hurt you. She's gonna be your guardian angel now. Okay?"

"Will I get to see her?"

"No sweetheart."

She laid her head on my shoulder, and I held her in my arms. I released her as she continued to hold me around my neck, and pulled the boys closer to me. They cried their eyes out for their little sister as Jayden joined us on the floor and put his arms around us all. "Come on, babies. I'm sure he's waiting on you guys."

"Okay," Garrett said.

I stood to get the boys an overnight bag packed while Alana made her way to Jayden's lap.

When we got to Jonathan's and had gotten out of the car, I noticed Jayden had stayed inside. Walking around to the passenger side of the car, I opened his door and said, "Come on. We won't be long."

His eyebrows lifted, then he got out of the car. He grabbed my hand, and we all walked to the back door. I was a little nervous to have Jayden with me, but this was my life, and I was gonna live it on my own terms. Now if I could only convince my heart of that, I'd be doing well. The boys knocked on the door, and Jonathan yelled, "Coming!"

When he swung the door opened, the kids sadly walked to him and embraced him. He smiled and said, "Hey, babies."

"Hi, Daddy," Alana said sadly.

"What's wrong, baby girl?"

"Bewan is an angel now. I can't play with her no more."

Jonathan swallowed hard and glanced up at me, then Jayden. "Yeah, but we'll get through this, okay?"

"Okay."

He stood to his feet. "Hey, Ansley. Thank you for bringing them."

He held his hand out to Jayden for a handshake. Jayden obliged. "I'm sorry for your loss."

"Thank you. Are y'all staying for a while?"

"No. I just wanted to bring the kids. I hope they can help keep you in good spirits."

"They will. The graveside service will most likely be Thursday if you can make it."

"Okay. Let me know for sure when you can, and I'll take a day off to make sure we attend."

"Okay. Thanks, Jayden, for coming."

Oh, I knew his ass was in his feelings for sure. The last he knew of, Jayden and I weren't even together anymore. Now, he was all welcoming. They shook hands again, then we turned to leave. "Bye kids. See y'all tomorrow evening."

"Okay, Mommy," they all said in unison.

I blew them kisses, and we left out the door. When we got to my car, Jayden grabbed my hand. "You wanna ride out to Houston with me?"

"Okay. What are we going do?"

"Well, I told my sister I would come visit her today. Now that I'm with you, I don't want to leave without you."

I smiled at him. "Okay. Sounds fun. She was nice."

"Yeah."

When we got back to my parents' house, I noticed they'd gotten home from their workout. As we walked in, Mama said, "Hey Ansley. Where are the kids?" When she saw Jayden, her eyebrows had risen. "Hi, Jayden! It's good to see you."

"Hey, Mrs. Pierre. Mr. Pierre. How are y'all?"

"We're good."

I answered my mama's question once they'd finished greeting one another. "Their baby sister died last night, Mama. They're with their daddy."

She put her hand to her mouth and tears filled her eyes. "That poor baby."

"I know."

Jayden sat on the sofa with my parents while I went to the room to get dressed. Before I could change, my phone was ringing. It was Jonathan. I answered immediately because I thought something had happened with the kids. "Hello?"

"So, y'all are back together?"

"What?"

"You and Jayden?

"Yeah. Why?"

"I just don't want us to have problems again."

"We won't have problems, only you. I love him Jonathan, and whether you wanna admit it or not, you know he's a good man. I refuse to let you fuck up my relationship with him because you butthurt. Concentrate on spending time with the kids, and quit worrying about what the fuck I do. That's no longer your concern. You got me?"

"Damn, Ans. I was just asking. I don't have a right to know that he's back in my children's lives?"

"Not really. You know my kids always come first, and I let you guilt trip me into that the last time. They love Jayden, and he treats them like they're his. So, if you wanna threaten to take me to court again, go on and do the shit."

I ended the call and flung my clothes to the bed, hot as shit.

ayden

WHEN ANSLEY CAME out the room in those tight-ass distressed jeans and halter top, it felt like I was salivating. I was in conversation with Mr. Pierre and had stopped mid-sentence. "Uh, Jayden? What were you saying?"

"Hell, I don't even know. Ansley, you look amazing, baby."

Mr. Pierre laughed and shook his head. I stood to my feet as she sauntered toward me. I pulled her in my arms. "Damn girl. We gon' have to make a pit stop before we go. A brother deprived as hell."

She giggled, then brought her lips to my ear. "I was hoping so."

Man, her lips grazed my ear, and I wanted to bust right there in front of her daddy. "Aight, Mr. Pierre. We're outta here."

He stood and shook my hand, then hugged Ansley. We made our way to my Range, and before she could get in, I pinned her against it and hungrily kissed her lips. Damn, I'd been needing that shit. I'd been wanting it ever since I first laid eyes on her early this morning. I slowly backed away from her and opened her door. Once she was in, I closed it and walked to the driver's side.

When I'd gotten in, Ansley had her hand between her legs, like she was holding herself. I frowned slightly. "You okay?"

"Yeah. My pussy is throbbing though."

"Oh, fuck, girl."

I bit my bottom lip then looked at my gray sweats. "Look what'chu did."

"Let's go, Jay."

I backed out of the driveway with the quickness as Ansley reached over and grabbed my package. I had a moment of déjà vu, but I pushed it out of mind. "Aww, fuck, baby. Don't start that shit, or we gon' end up fucking in this Range."

"Quit talking noise, Jay and get to the house."

I was driving as fast as I safely could. Ansley was so fucking expressive when it came to sex. She turned me on in every way. After about ten minutes of her laughing loudly at my driving, I was turning in the driveway. "You finna pay for that stunt you pulled. You 'bout to get two weeks' worth of fucking orgasms. I hope you ready."

"Make me pay for that shit, baby."

I gave her a one cheeked smile, then walked around the car and yanked her out, then threw her over my shoulder as she screamed with laughter. Even with her across my shoulder, I could feel how hot her pussy was. After unlocking the door, I placed her on her feet. Pulling her close to me, my lips touched every inch of her face, neck, and shoulders. Right there in the kitchen, I untied her halter and wrapped my lips around those gorgeous brown nipples.

Ansley moaned as I twirled my tongue around each one, then pushed them together and sucked them both simultaneously. "Oh shit, Jay."

"Mmm hmm," I moaned.

I released her breasts, then unbuttoned her pants. Picking her up, I sat her on the island and pulled off my shirt. My dick was standing at attention, begging for a dip inside of her hot box. I slid her pants off to see her pussy juicing in her underwear. The seat of her panties was so wet, it looked like she'd sat in a tub of water before putting her pants on.

I slid my pants off as she damn near ripped her panties off. My face went right where it was needed. That pearl was calling my name. Draping her thick-ass legs over my shoulders, I sucked her clit, making love to it with my tongue. She grabbed my head and pushed me in deeper as I slid my fingers inside of her. "Jay, I'm about to cum already."

I released her clit and said to her pussy, "Give it to me then."

Before I could put my mouth back on her, she'd came all on the granite. I dove back in as she squirmed, breathing heavily. Licking and slurping up all her goodness was making me weak with desire. The more I tasted her, the more I wanted, the more I craved. I slid my fingers inside of her once again, making the come here motion, hitting her G-Spot while I slid my other hand up her body and pinched her nipples. "Jay-deeeen!"

I almost came in my drawers the way she screamed my name. Her legs were trembling, and that creamy goodness was making its way to my tongue. I didn't stop. She was really squirming all over the countertop as I pulled her closer. This time I put my finger that was drenched in her juices in her ass. "I can't take it! Oh, fuck!"

"I told you I was gon' punish this pussy," I said barely above a whisper.

Going back to the task at hand, I sucked her clit until she was almost in a sitting position, clawing my back up. Once she came again, I pulled my drawers off and climbed on top of the island with her. I pushed inside of her quickly. I couldn't wait any longer. "Oh, fuck!"

Her shit was so damned hot and wet, I wanted to bust immediately. I was still for a moment, enjoying the way she felt. Letting my dick marinate in there. Slowly, I began stroking her pussy as I pushed her legs to her shoulders. "Jayden, yes baby."

"Ans, don't take this away from me again."

I leaned over her and hit her pussy with some deadly strokes. She screamed in ecstasy while pulling my face to hers. I kissed her lips then moved to her neck as I continued to fill her with dick. I began pumping faster and harder as she screamed, begging me for more. When I hit her with everything I had, she tried to scoot away. "Hell naw. Bring yo' ass back here, Ans."

I continued to pound into her as she screamed and came all over my dick. That was it though. I couldn't take much more. "Ansley fuck. Where you want this shit?"

She wouldn't answer me. I wanted to pull out, but I didn't. Hopefully, she was on the pill because I couldn't vacate this pussy until I'd released every drop inside of her. "Ansley! Fuck!"

I nutted inside of her, then slid off the countertop. She was so spent, but we weren't done yet. I pulled her off the countertop and led her to the sofa. I gently pushed her over the back of it and had my way with her, digging for buried treasure. She threw her ass back at me, twerking and cumming all on my dick, making me ejaculate prematurely. I turned her around and kissed her passionately.

When our kiss ended, she led me to the couch and straddled me, slow grinding on me until he rose to the occasion again. She guided me inside of her and rode that shit like it would be her last time. I held her tightly around her waist, then began pumping into her as she once again trembled to ecstasy. Her wetness was coating my balls and probably part of the sofa, but I didn't give a damn. "Jayden, fuck!"

After giving her a few more pumps, I nutted deep in her pussy. She collapsed against me as we panted and laid still until we recovered from that mind-blowing, love-making session.

"So, what happened to lunch, Jayden?" CiCi asked.

"Look, my baby needed me, and shit, I needed her. Dinner is just as good as lunch."

Cierra giggled as Ansley blushed. We'd met up at the Cheese-cake Factory and had dinner instead of lunch. Me and Ansley fell asleep on the sofa with her still straddled across my lap. We'd worn each other out. When we woke up, we'd been asleep almost two hours. By the time we got to Houston to meet up with Cierra, it was nearly six o'clock.

"Whatever, Jayden. How have you been, Ansley?"

"I've been good. What about you? How far along are you?"

"I've been good. I'm almost eighteen weeks already."

"Wow! Do you know what you're having?" Ansley asked excitedly.

CiCi glanced at me and said, "That's why I wanted you to come today."

She handed me an envelope. I frowned slightly, then opened the card. It was filled with drawings of stuffed animals, balloons, and pinks and blues. The writing was in calligraphy, and it was a simple four-lined poem. It read,

We've never met, but our time is coming soon.

I hope you have plans for me and plenty of toys

Loving you and you loving me will be a great joy.

So, get ready Uncle Jayden, I'm a boy!

I looked up at her and smiled. "I'm gonna have a nephew. Congratulations, CiCi."

"Thanks, Jayden. I'm happy for you too. I love seeing you two together. Ansley makes you so happy."

"That she does," I said, then smiled at Ansley and grabbed her hand.

We continued our dinner and talked more about CiCi's plans once the baby was born. She was making Ansley and me just as excited as she was. While we sat, Ansley's phone rang. She showed it to me, so I could see it was Jonathan, then rolled her eyes. "Hello?... Why?" She pulled the phone from her ear, then said, "Excuse me for just a minute."

I nodded as she got up from the table and walked outside. CiCi looked at me with knowing eyes. "How are you really? I can see something in your eyes right now that I don't really like."

"We just got back together today. Don't tell Mama, 'cause I don't wanna hear her shit."

"You know I won't."

"Ansley broke up with me two weeks ago, because her ex-husband is trying to give her hell. She wants me to stay out of it, but how can I? If he's talking to her crazy, I'm gon' jump in. Then he was upset that the kids were calling me daddy."

"Shit. How you gon' handle that?"

"She said she refused to let him control her anymore. She probably left out so she can curse him out."

"I see what Mama meant, though. She just wants what's best for you, Jay. None of us wanna see you hurt."

I closed my eyes briefly. I knew being with Ansley was a risk, but it was a risk I was willing to take. "I love her, CiCi. I'm worse without her and the drama than with her and all the bullshit that comes with it. I think this time around, though, she's all in."

"I hope you're right."

Shit, me too. The waitress came and delivered our cheesecake, and just as I was about to dig into mine, Ansley came back and flopped down next to me. "Everything okay?"

"Yeah. We'll talk on the way back."

She dug into her cheesecake as I noticed how red her face was. I glanced at CiCi as she gave me a worried look. Knowing what she was thinking, I averted my attention back to Ansley. "You sure you okay, Ans?"

She looked up at me, then gently rubbed her hand over my cheek. I could feel her calming down. "I'm okay, baby."

Leaning toward me, she kissed my lips, then went back to her cheesecake. She was trying to make me okay with her silence, but I was everything but. My nerves were on edge to know what this fuck-nigga had said now. I finished off the cheesecake in front of me as

CiCi talked about her classes coming up this fall. School was starting at the end of the month.

When we left, I didn't try to pull anything from Ansley. I knew when she was ready to talk, she would. We'd been driving for almost thirty minutes when she decided to say something. "Jay don't worry. I'm just angry. His punk ass gives me a headache. I didn't want to get out of pocket in front of Cierra."

"What happened?"

"He wanted me to come back to his house to watch a movie with them. I've already told him that you and I are back together. The crazy part about the shit is that he'd already told the kids that I was gonna come. Alana was crying in the background when I said I wasn't coming."

I shook my head slowly. "When is he gon' ever let go? I mean I know you're hard to let go of, but he needs to move around."

"Yes, he does. He irritates my entire soul. It's like he's trying to play on my sympathy because Belan died. When is this shit gonna end? I have to answer his calls when he has the kids."

"Don't answer the first call. If it's an emergency, he'll call right back. Or how about if it's an emergency, he can call your parents or me."

"That's a good idea, but I'm afraid he won't call anyone when it's something I need to know."

I didn't know what else to tell her about it, and honestly, I was tired of talking about the shit. Grabbing her hand, I brought it to my lips and kissed it. "We'll get through this. Hopefully, he'll eventually get the point."

nsley

IF I COULD MAKE Jonathan's ass disappear, I would in a heartbeat. He was threatening my sanity. Jayden was doing his best to keep me in a good head space, but I knew it would only be a matter of time before he got at Jonathan. Today was the graveside service, and Jayden was leaving work early to be with us. Jonathan had picked the hottest time of the day to have it. At one in the afternoon, we were all sure to be sweating.

My mama helped the boys get dressed in their khaki pants and short-sleeved, button-down polo shirts while I finished combing Alana's hair. I'd put a khaki dress on Alana to match her brothers and me. "You need any more help, baby?"

"No, Mama. I got it. Thank you."

"Okay. I'm going get the biscuits out of the oven."

"Okay."

My parents were also going to the graveside service. Everyone was going to show support for my babies. Remo had called me yesterday to inform me that he and Caricia would be there as well. He'd also said that he knew I felt sorry for Jonathan, but it was no longer my job to be there for him in that capacity. Jayden was who should matter the most. He didn't have to remind me of Jayden's worth, because I was well aware of it.

I just didn't want to feel cold and heartless by not being there for Jonathan. Remo made me feel more at ease about it though, and I was glad he'd called me. As I finished combing Alana's hair, I could hear the knock on the door. Shortly after, I could hear Jayden, Remo, and Caricia's voices. They'd all must have gotten here at the same time.

Alana ran to the kitchen as I quickly got dressed, putting on my khaki pants and dress shirt. When I walked to the front, I saw Jayden had on khakis too. "I see brilliant minds think alike," he said as Remo rolled his eyes.

"Remo don't be a hater all your life. Learn to appreciate greatness," Jayden said, pulling me closer to him. I kissed his cheek as he said, "You look great, baby."

"Thank you. So do you."

I kissed Caricia's cheek, then went to the kitchen to help the kids so we could go.

———

THE SERVICE WAS SO SAD. Ranika's parents were there, and they didn't seem to like Jonathan too much. They could join the club because there was a lot of people in that line. I was at the front of it. I didn't know how a man I loved for years, could be the man that I couldn't stand. Jayden came along so unexpectantly. He was everything Jonathan should have been to me as his wife. As we went to Jonathan's to drop the kids off to him, I couldn't help but to unbuckle and kiss him. "What was that for?"

"I just wanted to tell you how much I appreciate you. I love you, Jay."

"I love you too, baby," he said with a smile on his lips.

When we got to Jonathan's, there was a cop car there. I frowned, then turned to Jayden. Before I could say anything, Alana asked, "Daddy in trouble?"

"I don't know, baby. Let me see what's going on. Okay?

"Okay."

"I'll stay in here with the kids. Go ahead."

I kissed Jayden's lips, then got out and almost ran to the house. They were leading a man out in handcuffs. I'd seen him at the service, but his identity remained a mystery to me. Jonathan was sitting at the table with his head in his hands. "What's going on?"

"He said he was coming to talk to me. That's Ranika's real dad. That was her step-father with her mom at the graveside. We started tussling because he said I killed Ranika and Belan."

"They were in a car wreck. How are you responsible for that?"

"Ranika had been telling me she needed new tires, so I told her I would get them. I forgot. A blowout caused the wreck. They'd said she was hit by a car that ran the red light originally, but that wasn't the case. She lost control, and a car hit her. Although the other car's light was yellow, it isn't illegal to run a yellow light. Ranika had drifted into the intersection when she'd finally gained control."

"My God," I said, putting my hand to my mouth.

"So, he'd come here to make me pay. He'd offered to change her tires, but she told him that I was going to do it."

He shook his head slowly as the police made their way back to him for questioning. I walked back outside and had Jayden get out so I could fill him in. The kids didn't need to hear that someone was trying to hurt their daddy. When I told him everything, he stood there in shock. Hell, I was in shock myself.

Once the officers walked out, I went back inside. Jonathan looked at me with sad eyes, then said, "It's probably best if they aren't here today. I'm not in the right frame of mind. Let them know that I love them, and I'll get them tomorrow evening."

He walked away, down the hall to the bedroom. As much as I

wanted to console him, I didn't. It was bad enough that he had lost his daughter, but now he felt responsible. I walked out the door and made sure it was locked before closing it.

When I got to Jayden's Range, the kids were staring at me. "Your daddy said he loves y'all, but he's not feeling well. He said he would come and pick you up tomorrow evening."

Their faces saddened, so Jayden quickly added, "So, we're gonna get ice cream!"

Just that fast, they were screaming in excitement. I kissed his lips. "Thank you, baby."

———

As WE SAT at the park watching the kids play, we talked about where we thought our future was going. The kids were having a ball. We'd gone back to my parents' house for them to change, then brought them to get ice cream and go to the park. "If we progress like I think we will, I would love for you and the kids to move in with me after Christmas. What do you think?"

"I think we should take it one day at a time."

He nodded, then realization seemed to sweep over his face. "I'm sorry, baby. I feel you."

I didn't live with Jonathan until we'd gotten married. Although I have three kids, I wanted to wait until that time came, before I start preparing to move in with Jayden. I at least wanted to be his fiancée before I made that move. Although Christmas wasn't around the corner, I didn't want to make such a drastic commitment just yet. It was August, so we had time to see if our relationship was going to flourish even more than it already had. We continued talking until I heard someone say, "Jayden?"

He turned to the young woman, then stood. "Hi, Korliss. How are you?"

That was the lady he'd given his phone number to while we were apart. I wondered if they had been talking or if she had called since then. Jayden turned to me and held his hand out for mine. I stood and plastered on a smile. "Korliss, this is my girlfriend, Ansley. Babe, this is Korliss."

She had a firm expression on her face, so I held my hand out. "It's nice to meet you."

"Likewise," she said while shaking my hand.

She didn't seem too happy to be introduced to me, but what she didn't realize, was that the feeling was mutual. She looked back at Jayden. "I didn't mean to interrupt y'all. I just thought that it was you and wanted to say hello."

"Okay. It was good to see you."

"You too, Jayden." She turned to me, and her smile faded a little. "Again, it was nice meeting you. You're a lucky woman."

Oh yeah? I gave her a one-sided smile. "No, I'm a blessed woman. Luck is by happenstance. Nothing about what we share is by sheer coincidence. This was predestined. And he's a blessed man as well."

Her eyes narrowed. Oh, she didn't want this war. I didn't have the slightest issue fighting for what was mine. Jayden put his arm around me as Korliss and I had a silent stare down. She gave me a tight smile and walked away. Jayden grabbed my hand as he sat on the bench. "Are you sure nothing more happened between the two of you?"

"Positive. Just a conversation in HEB and a phone conversation."

He pulled me down in his lap and held me around my waist as I continued to watch her walk to her car. When she got there, she glanced up at us, then got in her car. "Okay. You know I don't mind roughing a bitch up."

He chuckled. "I know Sugar Ray. You have nothing to worry about."

I slapped his arm as he laughed, then pulled me into him. He began tickling me, and I laughed loudly while trying to get away from him. When he released me, I ran to the playground with the kids to help Alana on the monkey bars. Her brothers had already gone across, and she wanted to do it too. I held her by her waist as she went from one bar to the next.

She was so happy and so was I. Jayden wrapped his arms around my waist as I helped Alana across, then he kissed my neck. This felt so amazing like we were a family. However, I couldn't count out Jonathan's ability to try to destroy everything. I turned to Jayden and kissed his lips, once Alana had gotten across. "Jayden, I love you so much."

"I love you too, Ans. More than I love myself."

His phone started to ring, so he pulled away from me to see who was calling. I watched him roll his eyes, then he answered. "Hey Ma... I know. I'm sorry... Umm, okay. Let me check with Ans... I'll call you back."

I almost rolled my eyes, but I contained myself as I waited for him to tell me what she wanted. He took a deep breath. "She wants us to come to dinner again tomorrow night. She said she was sorry how things went last time, and she wanted to make it up to us and just start over."

He stared into my eyes. I could see that he wanted me to work this out with his mother. So, I said, "Okay. But I'm doing this for you."

Pulling me in his arms, he kissed me long on the lips. "Thank you, Ans. Hopefully, she's gotten her act together."

"I'll do anything for you, Jay. I know she was looking out for you."

"She was, but she didn't have to be rude to you because of that."

"Mommy!" Alana yelled.

I turned to see her watching us. A grin was on her face, so I knew she was about to say something silly. "Yes, Alana?"

She walked closer to us. "You wove Jayden?"

I smiled, then looked in his eyes. "I sure do, baby."

"Mommy and Jayden sitting in a tree, K-I-S-S-I-N-G..." the boys sang.

I giggled as Jayden stared at me with a smirk on his face. He bit his bottom lip, then kissed me while the kids laughed and clapped.

When he broke the kiss, I hugged him tightly. "Mama, are you and Jayden getting married?" Sage asked.

I looked at him, then Jayden. "One day, baby."

The love I felt from Jayden at that moment was indescribable. It felt all-consuming, and I loved the feeling. Before he could respond, the bottom fell out. Rain poured on us as the kids screamed in excitement. That was Beaumont weather for you. One minute it was sunny, then pouring the next. Jayden scooped up Alana, and we ran to his truck.

Once we'd all gotten in, Garrett yelled, "That was fun!"

We laughed, then went back to my parents' house. I wished I didn't have to work tomorrow. I just wanted to lay in Jayden's arms tonight. It was like our relationship had grown so much stronger just from our conversation. We held hands and glanced at one another the entire ride there.

When we walked through the door, my dad laughed. "I see y'all got caught in the five-minute show."

Jayden laughed. "Yes. Ruined the kids' playtime."

"Come on, babies. Let's get these wet clothes off you."

The boys were jumping around excitedly, and Alana looked miserable. I giggled and led them to the bathroom. I started the water in the bathtub, then said, "Boys, go get you some pajamas."

"Aww. We have to go to bed?" Garrett asked.

"Not yet, but we aren't going anywhere else, so you might as well put on your bedclothes."

"Okay," Sage said.

I brought Alana to my parents' bedroom and found my mama laying in the bed. It was only six. "Mama, you feel okay?"

"Yeah, I was just tired."

I could tell in her eyes, that it was something more. She probably didn't want to talk about it in front of Alana. "Okay. Well, we're gonna use your bathroom."

"Okay."

I didn't like seeing her this way. She was always upbeat about everything. After getting Lana cleaned up and towel drying her hair, I sent her to meet Jayden and my dad. Once she left the room, I closed the door. "What's going on, Mama?"

She sat up in the bed, and I could tell that she'd been crying. "I know how you feel now."

I frowned slightly. "What do you mean?"

"I found out that your dad had an affair with Caricia's mother eight years ago."

I dropped my head. I never wanted her to find out, neither did Remo. "I'm sorry, Mama. How did you find out?"

"He told me. He said it's been eating at him for years, and that when Remo met Caricia, it really came to the forefront of his mind. He didn't want to see me hurt, but he said it felt like he'd been even more deceitful by not making me aware of his downfall."

Damn. I couldn't believe he did that. I sat next to my mama and pulled her in my arms as she'd done to me on so many occasions. "I'm so sorry, Mama."

"It's okay. I just need some time to get over the betrayal. I know he was sincere. He didn't have to tell me. We will just move on from here, but I told him I needed time."

"What did he say?"

"He said he understood."

"I hate that he told you because I never wanted to see you hurt. But I respect him for telling you also."

"Yeah, me too. I love that man in there so much, it just hurts to know that at some point in his life, I wasn't enough."

That line was so familiar. It was the same mental state I was in when I found out Jonathan was cheating on me. "I know how you're feeling, Mama. Daddy is a good man, though. He had a moment of weakness. Whenever you need to talk, just know I'm here for you. I love you, Mama."

"Thank you, baby. I love you too."

I smiled at her, then went to the hallway bathroom to make sure the boys were done. When I opened the door, they yelled, "Mommy!"

When they covered their private parts, I knew they were growing up. "I'm sorry, boys."

I closed the door and leaned against the wall with my hand on my chest. They weren't babies anymore. Walking down the hall to the front room, I saw Alana sitting on Jayden's lap, playing with his ears. I think she was crushing on my man. Daddy was smiling at them, but I could see the sadness in his eyes. I was the one that had walked in on him and Caricia's mother.

I'd kept their secret after he promised me it wouldn't happen again. When Remo started dating Caricia, and I met her and her mother in Chuck's Sandwich Shop, I knew it wouldn't be good. I'd recognized Mrs. Edwards right off. I could never forget her face, and Caricia looked just like her. She'd been the love of my daddy's life before my mama and had left him due to her own insecurities.

I sat next to my daddy and grabbed his hand. "I respect you even more, Daddy. I love you."

"I love you too. Although I knew it would hurt her, I also knew it was the right thing to do."

I leaned my head on his shoulder, and he put his arm around me. My daddy wasn't perfect, but he was trying to be. I loved that about him, and it was what I loved about Jayden. "Alana, can we switch spots?"

"Nope. Jayden mine."

My eyebrows had risen along with his. I knew she was trying to steal my man. She hugged his neck tightly as he and daddy laughed. I walked over to them. "Umm lil girl. That's my man. Now move."

She poked her lip out but slid off Jayden's lap as he stared up at me. I stood directly in front of him, and he licked his lips. He pulled me down in his lap and kissed my neck. Alana had sat next to my daddy and had crossed her arms across her chest. Jayden chuckled, then said, "Come on, lil mama."

She jumped from the sofa and ran to his arms. My daddy shook his head as Alana climbed in Jayden's lap. "I'm going check on your mama," Daddy said while standing to his feet.

"Okay, Daddy."

Alana and I both laid on Jayden as he wrapped his arms around us. "I love my girls."

"We love you too," I said.

We loved him more than words could express. My baby girl wanted whatever I wanted. She saw me happy, and as young as she was, she realized Jayden was one of the reasons why. I believed that was why she was so attached to him. For that, I would be forever grateful to Jayden. He was showing my daughter how a woman should be treated.

ayden

GOING to this dinner was making me nervous. Ansley and I were going to be dropping the kids to Jonathan's before we went to my parents' house. I just hoped there was no drama with him today. Usually, drama was a good reason for me to stop fucking with somebody, but Ansley was worth far too much to me to let go.

When we got to Jonathan's house, I helped them get their bags and my lil mama said, "Bye Jayden."

"See you later, lil mama."

I stooped down and she ran to my arms as Ansley rolled her eyes. I hugged her tightly and kissed her cheek. Alana giggled as I said, "Ans, don't be jealous of Lana and me."

She rolled her eyes again, then winked. Damn, I loved that woman. I shook the boys' hands, and they went to the door. I got back in the Range. It seemed to be taking Jonathan a while to come to the door though. Ansley looked back at me with a worried look on her face. She pulled her phone from her pocket. The garage door was open, so we knew he was here.

After she put her phone back in her pocket, the door opened. Ansley glanced back at me before walking inside. I didn't know what was going on, but I could see the sadness on her face. My gut was telling me to get out the Range, so I did. When I got to the door, Ansley was opening it. "I was just about to come and get you."

"What's going on?"

"I'm at a crossroads. He's clearly depressed. I don't know if I should leave the kids."

"You know him better than anyone. Do you think the kids being here will help him?"

"I know him well, but I've never seen him this depressed. So, I really don't know Jay. Come in."

I walked in the house to see Jonathan sitting on the sofa with Alana in his lap. She was laying on his chest as he kissed her forehead repeatedly. When he saw me, he stood, holding Alana in his arms. I walked over and shook his hand. "I'm so sorry, man."

The man in front of me seemed like an empty shell. I couldn't imagine what it was like losing a child, nor did I want to. "Thank you."

He sat back on the couch. I pulled Ansley to the side. "Let's get them all something to eat. I think it will do him some good for them to stay."

I glanced back over to them to see him rolling a car on the floor with the boys while Alana sat on his shoulders. I smiled slightly as she covered his eyes, and he smiled. The kids would be therapeutic for him. "I think you're right, Jay."

"If you want, you can stay here while I go get food."

"No, I'm coming with you."

I smiled at her. "Okay, let's go."

While she asked what they wanted to eat, I called my mama to let her know we would be a little late. She seemed to understand. "McDonald's," Ansley said, shaking her head slowly.

"Ans."

We both turned around to see Jonathan holding out $30. "I got it, Jonathan," she said.

We left out, and I opened her door. After I backed out the driveway, Ansley said, "Thank you, babe. I'm sorry we're going to be late for dinner. Your mama really won't like me after this."

"Hey, look at me."

She looked at me with sad eyes. I grabbed her hand. "If my mama can't understand this situation, then she's the one with the problem. You have the biggest heart, and I admire you for that."

"Thank you, baby. You have a big heart too. I appreciate you more than you know."

After we got the food back to Jonathan and the kids, we headed to dinner. When I drove in the driveway, we were only fifteen minutes late. If she tripped on that, we were going to leave immediately. I helped Ans out, and we walked to the back door. As soon as I knocked, Mama was opening the door. "Hey! Y'all come in. I thought y'all were gonna be later."

I released the breath I was holding, then smiled and kissed my mama's cheek. When she got to Ansley, she pulled her in her arms. "Hi Ansley. Thank you for coming."

Ansley nodded. "Yes, ma'am. Thank you for inviting me."

We walked to the front room where my step-dad was. "Y'all made it." He stood and shook my hand, then Ansley's. "Where are the kids? I was looking forward to seeing them again."

Ansley smiled. "They're with their dad this weekend."

"Oh okay. They are very well-mannered. I applaud you for that. Y'all come on to the table."

"Thank you," Ansley said as she blushed.

Now, this was how this shit should have gone the first time. I led Ansley to the table and pulled out her chair. Mama smiled at me as Ansley sat. After scooting her chair in, then sitting next to her, she kissed my cheek. I held her hand as Mama said, "Ansley, I owe you an apology. I was rude to you the last time you were here. It's not in my character to be that way, and I'm sorry."

"It's okay. I know you're just looking out for Jay, but I promise you, that I love him as much as he loves me."

Mama smiled. "Well, that settles it."

We all grabbed hands as Daddy blessed the food. It wasn't a big fancy meal like last time. She'd made spaghetti and meatballs, along with salad and garlic toast. We dug in, and the conversation continued, allowing them to get to know Ansley, and her getting to know them. My phone started ringing though, so I pulled it from my pocket to see it was Korliss.

Why was she calling me? It ain't like we had even established a friendship before I got back with Ansley. I silenced it as Ansley watched me. By the expression on her face, I knew she'd seen who was calling. My mama looked from me to her. "Everything okay?"

"Yes, ma'am. Everything's cool," I said, pulling Ansley close to me. I leaned over to her ear. "I'll let you call her back when we get to the car."

She smirked at me, and I kissed her lips. Putting her hand on my thigh, she squeezed it as she inched higher. I didn't know why she wanted to start that. She had no idea that I would definitely have her blushing in front of my parents. "Aight, don't start nothing, girl."

She quickly pulled her hand away and stared at me. I laughed loudly as my mama frowned. "Jayden, I know you ain't being nasty at my dinner table."

"That was Ansley!" I yelled as Ansley slapped my arm.

"Really Jayden?"

"Jayden, it was you. I know you. Take that nasty shit to your house."

My mouth hung open while Ansley laughed. "That's just so wrong, Ma."

We continued dinner and actually had a great time. Mama and Ansley actually walked off and was having their own private conversation. I sat with Daddy as he watched TV. "Daddy, how's Daniel? I haven't talked to him in a long time."

"He's good. His wife was pregnant, but she miscarried."

"Damn. I'm gon' have to call him. When was the last time you talked to him?"

"I just talked to him yesterday. The time difference is what keeps us from talking as much. It's a seven-hour difference in Germany."

"Yeah, I know. By the time I get off, they're sleeping. I'll have to make it a point to call on my off day."

I hadn't talked to my older step-brother, Daniel in at least four months. He had a wife and a five or six-year-old son. We weren't as close as me and CiCi were, but we were close, nevertheless. We'd been sitting there for a few minutes when my phone started ringing again. I had a feeling it was Korliss again. As I pulled it from my pocket, I saw it was her.

She was tripping for real. I ain't ever had a chick that I hadn't slept with sweat me that hard. Silencing the call, I looked up to see Ansley watching me. They'd made it back to us. Korliss was gon' have to be stopped. I ain't even done shit, and she got Ansley looking at me sideways. She sat next to me. "That her again?"

"Yeah."

"You sure y'all didn't fuck?" she said low in my ear.

"I'm positive, baby. I ain't do nothing but talk to her. She tripping, though."

"Yeah, she is. But I'm 'bout to be tripping too. You introduced her to me, so now she just being straight up disrespectful."

Ansley had gotten a little louder, and my dad had turned to look at us. I took a deep breath. "Why don't we go call her now, so we can enjoy the rest of the evening, baby."

"I thought you would never ask," she said, standing to her feet.

Aww shit. I stood as well and shook my daddy's hand. When mama came back to the room, she had a movie in her hand. Her eyes were wide when she saw us leaving. "Aww, y'all are leaving already?"

"I'm sorry, Mrs. Jacobs, but yes ma'am. Remember your nasty son," Ansley said.

My head whipped around to her so fast, I damn near gave myself whiplash. "Ansley! That's my mama."

"And? She obviously knows you're nasty."

I slapped her ass, then pulled her close. "You gon' pay for that."

"Alright, alright. Y'all get outta here. Ansley call me sometimes."

"Yes, ma'am."

When we walked out, that smile fell right off Ansley's face. I ain't ever seen her flip the script like that. Opening her door, she stood close to me and pulled my phone from my pocket. Here we go. I walked around to my side and got in. "After I finish this conversation with this bitch, she getting blocked."

"I don't have a problem with that, Ans."

She put the phone on speaker as it rang, then gave it to me. My eyes widened for a minute, but then I realized she wanted to hear what Korliss wanted. "Hello?"

"You called me?"

"Jayden, why didn't you answer? I wanted to ask how serious you and your girl were. You just seem so nice, and I don't wanna miss out on an opportunity to get to know you."

That was that. Ansley took the phone from me. "This is what you ain't gon' do. I need you to listen to what I'm about to say because next time I won't be talking. Jayden is mine. His heart, his mind, his soul, and his dick. Every part of him belongs to me. You got me, bitch?"

She was quiet as hell, but I knew she hadn't hung up. Ansley looked at me, then back at the phone. "You can stay quiet, but I know you hear me. If there is a next time, I'm gon' find you and drag yo' ass. Don't let my looks fool you. I will fuck you up over this man right here. Make this yo' last time trying to contact him."

I watched Ansley go in my phone and block her number. She handed it back to me. "Jayden, you wouldn't hurt me, right?"

"Ans... Don't let her make you doubt my character. I'm only

yours. I haven't slept with nobody else since before Christmas last year before we were even a couple." Her eyes widened slightly. "You the only woman I want. I would never hurt you, baby. You mean everything to me."

"I'm sorry, Jayden."

"You don't have to apologize, baby. I'm about to take you home and show you just how much I need you, desire you, and crave you. It feels like my soul ascends into heaven whenever I'm with you. So you know how that feels, when we get to my house, I'm gon' make that body levitate."

"Damn, Jay. Hurry up, shit."

———

I HAD TO WORK SATURDAY, but as soon as I got off, I made a beeline to my baby. The kids were still with their dad. I was off tomorrow and Monday. I'd take that shit too. The kids would be starting school next Monday, so I wanted to spend all day Monday with them. I'd planned to take them to the zoo in Houston, then to Schlitterbahn in Galveston. Ansley was talking about taking off Monday so she could be with us.

Ansley was already at my house. She'd spent the night last night. There was no way I was letting her leave me. We'd christened every room in my house, every piece of furniture, and every countertop in the place. We were so damned tired, we'd gone to sleep sticky as hell. When I woke up this morning, I rolled over right into that pussy.

Then we'd gone to the shower, and I had my way with her in there too. Ansley was so tired after our shower, I literally carried her back to the bed. She'd called me around lunchtime to tell me she was cooking dinner. As usual, I was starving and couldn't wait to get there and see what she cooked. When I got in the driveway, I frowned at the other vehicle parked there. It looked like Jonathan's car.

What the fuck was he doing in my house without me being home? That was some disrespectful shit since we didn't really know each other like that. However, when I maneuvered around his car, I noticed he was sitting on my back porch. Alone. Hmm. I wondered what this was about. This had to be a friendly visit.

I got out of my Range, then made my way to the back door. He stood when he saw me. He looked a lot better than he did Friday. As I walked up the stairs, he held his hand out. I shook it, then he said, "Hi Jayden. I hate to infringe on your time with Ans, especially after you just got off, but I wanted to talk to you."

"Okay," I said, standing there waiting to hear what he had to say.

"Oh, I'll wait for you to greet her and the kids."

My eyebrows had risen slightly. "Um, okay. You wanna come in?"

"Well, I wanted to talk to you in private, so I'll stay out here."

"Okay, well, I'll be right back."

What was this nigga up to? I went inside to see Ansley walking away from the window. "Hey, baby. How was your day? What's Jonathan doing here? I thought he wasn't bringing the kids until tomorrow."

I kissed her lips as I heard little feet running through the house. "Jayden!"

"What's up, lil mama?"

I stooped to kiss her cheek. She'd learned not to hug me while I had my Nomex on. I went to the washroom and took them off. I always wore shorts and a t-shirt underneath them. When I came back out, Alana, Sage, and Garrett were standing at the door waiting on me. I shook the boys' hands and rubbed their curly mohawks, then picked my baby girl up. She hugged my neck, then whispered, "Daddy's here."

I chuckled. "I know. I'm about to go talk to him."

Ansley hugged me. I let Alana down so I could greet my baby properly. Making sure the kids were all gone, I grabbed her ass and put my lips to hers. "He said he needed to talk to you, and he won't tell me what it's about. They were on their way to the water park in Lumberton and decided to stop here, before going."

"Hmm. Okay. Well, I'll be back."

She giggled nervously, then brought her nosy ass back to the window. I walked out the door. "Jonathan, you want something to drink?"

"Naw, I'm good. Thanks."

I sat in the chair next to him, waiting to hear what he had to say. "I know you're wondering what I'm doing here, but I needed to talk to you." He paused for a moment, then continued. "Ansley and I met at the beginning of ninth grade. She was the prettiest girl in school. Everybody wanted her to be their girlfriend."

"I can see that."

He smiled slightly. "When she said yes to me, I was the happiest boy on campus. We dated all during high school. When it was time to go to college, Ansley chose to stay here and go to Lamar. I was offered a basketball scholarship to three schools. Neither of those schools was Lamar. I wanted to go to Florida State so bad, but I loved Ansley so much, I couldn't see myself leaving her behind."

I didn't know where this talk was going, but I was hoping he'd hurry up and get to the point. "When we were twenty-one, I asked her to marry me. She planned our wedding for a date after we graduated. Things couldn't be better. We rarely argued, and when we did, it was never a serious argument. When we got married, we'd both graduated, and I was working for the City of Beaumont. She hadn't found a job yet. We had the perfect relationship. A month later she found a job and the same day she started working, we found out she was pregnant.

"Our life was perfect. We had our twins and two almost three years later when I found out Ansley was pregnant again, I was ecstatic. After Alana was born, things were still great. Somehow though, when Alana was almost two, I got caught up with Ranika. She was a temp in the water department. It started out being friendly exchanges. Then it turned into more.

"Seeing how easy it was to fool around with her, attracted me to her even more. Before I knew it, I had cheated on Ansley. That woman meant everything to me. Even after she found out I was cheating, she stayed. Once I was exposed, things went downhill. It was like I expected her to take that gut-check and not suffer from it. She was supposed to forgive me, and everything was supposed to go back to normal."

He shook his head. "You obviously saw the outcome of all that. After I found out Ranika was pregnant, I knew I would lose Ansley. That tore me to pieces, but I had no one to blame but myself. When she left, I thought that if I took care of her and the kids, she would eventually take me back. When she started dating you, it was like a slap in my face. Although she never sold me a wolf ticket, I still thought I had a chance."

I remained quiet, just listening to him. Sitting up in his chair, he continued, "I started making life miserable for Ans. I was trying to force her to stay in my life. In that process, it caused her to mistreat you, and I'm sorry. I didn't know how to let her go. When the kids started calling you daddy, I blamed her for it, instead of pointing the blame at myself.

"Ansley is so happy right now, and I know it's because of you. I came here to be a man and tell you, I'm letting go. As bad as that hurts, she's not mine anymore and hasn't been for a long time. You're good to her, and if she's happy, I'm happy. I respect you for how you take care of her and my kids. You are like a dad to them. They see you more than they see me. I realized that I shouldn't be offended that they wanna call you dad. It doesn't negate the role I play in their life.

"You're just as good to them as I am, and I couldn't ask for a better man to be in my kids' life. So, I thought it was only right that I came here like a man and apologized to you for the bullshit with Ansley and to thank you for taking care of the family I neglected."

His eyes were full, and I was just waiting for the tears to fall. I held my hand out to him and shook it. "I appreciate that, Jonathan. I just want you to know that you never have to worry about your babies. I consider them my babies too. I'm gonna always treat them like they're mine."

"They are yours, Jayden. They belong to the three of us."

He stood from his chair, so I did as well. We walked inside, and Ansley was standing near the window. She had a smile on her face, and her eyes looked like they were about to overflow the abundances of her heart. Jonathan called for the kids, and Ansley walked to him and hugged him. "Thank you, Jonathan."

"You don't need to thank me for something I should've done a long time ago. Thank you for always being a good person. Jayden you're a blessed man."

I draped my arm around Ansley's shoulders. "Yes, I am."

The kids came to the front. "Bye Mommy! Bye Jayden!" Alana yelled.

"Bye, lil mama. See you tomorrow."

We watched them from the porch as they waved bye. Once they'd left the driveway, Ansley looked at me and said, "I feel so damn free, and it feels amazing."

"Me too. It wasn't that I wanted his approval, but I did want his acceptance of the situation. Now that he's gotten it, I wanna make love to you right on this porch."

Ansley giggled. "Peace. I can finally have peace. And you can make love to me wherever you want to."

She pulled her shirt over her head, and I immediately teased her nipples through her bra. I scooped her in my arms as she laughed. This love-making session was gon' be out of this world. "Come on, let's go flying."

nsley

"Alana, wait! You wanna get lost?"

We'd just gotten to the Houston Zoo, and Alana had gone into auto-pilot. Full speed ahead. Jayden picked her up and sat her on his shoulders. I'd taken off work today to enjoy time with Jayden and my babies. The new school year would be starting next week, and Jayden wanted the kids to have a great time on his last off day before their first day. He wouldn't be off again until that day. The boys were excited as well. They were starting first grade, and Alana would still be home. She would start Pre-K next school year.

As much as I tried to discourage it, Remo and Caricia had come along as well. I didn't know how I felt about her walking around the zoo all day. She was twenty-two weeks, and it was hot outside. Before leaving Beaumont, we decided we would save Schlitterbahn for another trip. I told Jayden there was no way we could do both in one day.

"Mommy, look! Monkeys!"

"I see, baby girl!"

Alana was so excited. The boys were excited as well, but they were trying to hide just how much. The monkeys were hopping all around, and I watched Alana's little hazel eyes follow them all over. "I can see we will be making a trip back here, sooner rather than later," Jayden said.

"I'm almost positive we will be."

Jayden put his arm around me, and we continued through the zoo, having a great time.

By the time we'd seen practically everything, it was almost five. I was starving, and so were the kids. Caricia looked tired as hell. Remo picked her up and cradled her in his arms as we walked to the car. "Aww, Uncle Me-mo picked up Aunt Weesh," Alana said.

"Just like I picked you up, huh?" Jayden asked.

She giggled as we continued walking. I held the boys' hands as we took what seemed like a mile trek to where we'd parked. "Mommy, we had fun today. Thank you," Sage said.

"Yes, we did! Thank you, Mommy and Daddy," Garrett added.

"You're welcome, babies."

I smiled and swallowed the lump in my throat as I thought about Jonathan. I'd heard every word he told Jayden the other day, and it moved my heart. To listen to him speak so passionately about me and how good of a woman I was, helped restore my self-confidence in a way. Jayden had helped with that, but it was like to hear it from Jonathan, the man that tore me down, did things for me that I'd never imagined it would.

Hearing Garrett revert back to calling Jayden daddy, let me know that Jonathan had also spoken to them about it. Jayden's chest was so puffed up, and he had the biggest smile on his face. "Mommy, Daddy said we can call Jayden daddy again if we wanted to," Sage said.

"He did? Why?"

"He said that he thought when we wanted to call Jayden daddy, that we didn't love him anymore. He said he knows we love him now and he was glad that we loved Jayden too."

I put my hand to my chest, then hugged my boys. Just as my emotions were about to get to me, Alana yelled, "But I said you were Mr. Incwedible!"

I shook my head and rolled my eyes. Jayden laughed, then pulled her off his shoulders and tickled her. They were two peas in a pod. Remo smiled as he looked on, then said to the kids, "Y'all are so special and blessed. You have two daddies that love you so much."

He sat Caricia on her feet, then put his arm around me. I quickly swiped the tear away that escaped. "We got two daddies!" Alana reiterated. "I love you, Daddy."

"I love you too, lil mama."

My heart couldn't get any fuller. We'd gotten to the car, and after the kids got in the Range, I turned my back and let the tears out that I couldn't seem to control. Remo helped Caricia in the car, then came and hugged me. I hugged my brother back. "Don't cry, Ans. I know they're tears of joy though."

"Me-mo, I'm so happy. I never thought this day would get here. Jonathan gave me hell for the past seven months. I'm so glad God softened him. I know it had something to do with losing Ranika and Belan, but regardless of how painful that was for him, it made him better."

"It did."

Jayden walked around the car and saw me crying. He immediately came to me as Remo let me go. "Everything okay, baby?"

"Yeah. I'm just happy." I wrapped my arms around him as he did the same to me. "I love you so much, Jayden."

"I love you too, Ans."

He kissed my forehead. Little miss bossy put her window down. "Mommy, I hungry!"

We all laughed as I wiped my face, then kissed Jayden's lips. "Let's go, baby before I have to hurt your BFF."

Jayden laughed. "Aight, watch yo'self. That's my baby."

We all got in the car and headed to Peter Piper Pizza. The minute we turned in the parking lot, the kids went crazy. They should have been tired, but they were ready to play. After ordering our pizza, Jayden and Remo took the kids to play, while Caricia and I sat at a table. "I told yo' ass, you shouldn't have come. I see you holding your stomach, Reesh. You okay?"

"Yeah. I'm just tired and hungry."

"That baby ain't playing with yo' lil ass. She gon' be bigger than you!"

She smiled brightly as she continued to rub her stomach. I stood and brought another chair to her so she could put her feet up. "Oh, that feels better. Thank you, Ans."

"You're welcome."

I kissed her cheek, then went back to my seat. "I'm so happy things worked out with you and Jayden. I've never seen him this happy."

"Me too. I love him more than I ever thought I was capable of loving anyone, other than my babies and Jonathan. It was hard, but well-worth the adversity."

"He's a good guy. Always has been."

"Yes, he is. So, have y'all come up with a middle name for Miss Teagan?"

"Girl, not yet. Remo wants her middle name to be Star."

"Star?" I asked with a frown.

"She'll be the star to his night. Since Night is his middle name."

"He so damned cheesy. You gon' name Teagan, Star?"

"I'm thinking about it. You know Remo's my baby, and I can't tell him no for too long."

I rolled my eyes as she laughed. They called our number to get our pizzas so I went up front to get them. Jayden met me as Remo corralled the kids. We got everything back to the table, then blessed the food and dug in. "Remo, what is this you wanna name baby girl?" I asked to pick with him.

"Teagan Star Pierre."

I rolled my eyes dramatically as Jayden laughed. "Bruh, Star?"

"What's wrong with it? She gon' be the twinkling lil star in my night. You can't tell me that ain't sweet for my baby girl."

"Whatever. I'm gon' call her Tea. She gon' live up to that name too. I'm gon' teach her to spill all the tea," I said.

"Tea?" Alana asked with a frown on her face.

"You stay over there and out of grown folks' conversation," I said to her.

"You wanna talk about my lil Star, but that's your six-bit change, right there," Remo said as he rubbed Caricia's belly.

"That's alright. I can handle her, though. I wanna see you handle a lil girl, Remo. She gon' have you wrapped around her pinky, just like Alana has Jayden."

"Hey, this ain't about me," Jayden added.

We all laughed, including Alana. She put her arm around his neck, pizza and all. "I love you, Daddy."

She kissed his cheek leaving pizza sauce on it, as we all said, "Aww."

"Y'all hush," Jayden said as Alana wiped the sauce off his cheek.

We continued to laugh and eat our pizza. I was glad I had taken off work today. My soul felt glad, and my heart was light.

———

When we got back to Beaumont, it was almost nine o'clock. Jayden helped me get the sleeping kids inside, then he went home. He had to go to work tomorrow, and he had to be there a lot earlier than what I had to be to work. I ran bath water for the boys, then knocked on my parents' bedroom door to see if I could bathe Alana in there. "Come in."

No one was in bed, but when I walked in further, I saw them sitting on the couch, Daddy holding Mama in his arms. "Aww, Gandpa wove Gandma."

Alana could never hold in what she was feeling. She always had to verbalize it, and I loved that about her. I kissed her cheek as my parents smiled. "I just wanted to see if I could bathe this little dirt goblin in your bathroom."

"Of course, Ansley," my dad said. "How was the zoo?"

"It was fun!" Alana yelled.

"Good! I'm glad you enjoyed it, baby girl."

Daddy stood from the couch, then leaned over and kissed Mama's forehead and left the room. After starting Alana's bath water and getting her undressed, I walked back to my mama. She was sitting on the couch still, with a smile on her face. "You okay, Mama?"

"Yes. Thank you, Ansley, for helping me through this. I was having a rough moment, but your dad just held me through it all."

"And that's what he should do, Mama. Although he's the one that hurt you, he needs to be the one that helps you heal."

"You're right, and we are getting through it together."

"Wun, ducky, wun!"

I kissed her cheek, then went back to the screaming little girl in the bathroom. "Alana, ducks can't run in water, they swim."

She giggled. "He was wight here on side the tub, Mommy."

I shook my head slowly. "Okay, baby. Let's get you cleaned up. It's past our bedtime."

"Mommy, Uncle Me-mo say I have two daddies."

"Yes, he did say that. You agree?"

"Huh?"

"Do you think you have two daddies?"

"Yes!" she said with a big smile on her face. "Mommy, I help Daddy feel better."

"You did? How?"

"He say because I love him. I'm his baby."

I smiled at her, then washed her up. "You are my baby too."

"But Mommy, Bewan is baby."

"I know, but Belan is in heaven."

"I saw her last night."

I looked in her innocent eyes. "What was she doing?"

"She fly, Mommy. And she pway with me."

"Played?"

"Yes!"

I knew that kids' innocence allowed them to see things we as adults couldn't sometimes. God was comforting my baby. "That's great, baby."

"Mommy, you have 'notha baby?"

"Ooh, I don't think so, sweetheart. Now, come on so you can get ready for bed."

I'd never thought to ask Jayden if he wanted kids of his own. I mean, seeing how much he loved mine, I was almost sure he did. If so, I'd be willing to have one or two with him. He was everything I needed. He was patience, love, compassion, and sincerity all rolled up in one. What more could I ask for?

EPILOGUE

hree months later

J AYDEN

"I'm so glad y'all were able to conceive again, Dan. Besides the weather, how is it in Germany? Are y'all coming back anytime soon?"

"Don't tell Daddy and Mama, but we plan to be there for Christmas."

"Aww man, that'll be great. I can't wait for you to meet my family."

"Family? You got married?"

"Naw, but I plan to propose soon. She has a set of twin boys that I love and little girl that I adore. I've never been happier."

"I can hear it in your voice. I'm happy for you, bruh."

"Thanks. Well, I have to go. I'm almost to the house."

"Okay. Well, hopefully, I'll see y'all in the next couple of weeks."

"Aight, bruh. Love you."

"Love you too."

I'd finally taken the time out to call my brother in Germany. That call was expensive as hell, but he was worth it. Things had been going well. Ansley and my mama were so close now, I had to hunt her down to spend time with her and my baby, Alana. It was always the boys and me. That was okay though. I was glad that they finally got over the awkwardness my mama had created.

Cierra had just graduated a week ago, and she was seven months pregnant. She'd made it to town and had been spending a lot of time with Mama, Ansley, and sometimes, Caricia. They were practically at the same spot in their pregnancy. CiCi had chosen to name the baby Crimson Onyx Knighton. His father had finally come around and had accepted that he would have a son. I was glad that he did. Hopefully, he would be as involved as he planned to be.

Jonathan had been doing well also. We even invited him out to the house a couple of times for dinner. It was also planned that he would be there on Christmas day when the kids opened their presents. He'd been going to a counselor to help with his depression. He and I had been talking quite often, and I was glad for the bond we shared through the kids.

Things had no choice but to go well when the three of us got along and were on one accord when it came to how we reared them. Ansley was still living with her parents, but whenever I was off on the weekends, they stayed with me if the kids weren't with Jonathan. I desperately wanted her to move in with me, but she'd made it perfectly clear that she wouldn't be until we moved to the next level in our relationship. She said she wasn't rushing me, because she was in no hurry, but that was where she stood on the subject. Hell, I felt rushed, though, and I loved that shit. I wanted her and the kids with me every day.

I wanted to marry her one day anyway, so she was gonna get one of her Christmas gifts early. I didn't want to do it in front of everybody. I needed her authentic reaction, and most importantly, I didn't want her to say yes because everyone was watching. If she wasn't ready, I wanted her to tell me that. My hands were trembling as I got to the house. I'd had to take a ride to try to calm my nerves.

Ansley was off today for some reason that I didn't remember, so she said she would come over. When she got there, I was so nervous about what I was gonna do, I made an excuse to leave. Now that I was back, my nerves had picked up once again. When I walked in, Ansley was moving around the kitchen, like she was preparing to cook something, as I slid my hands in the pockets of my sweat pants.

"Hey, baby. You okay?" she asked, then kissed my lips.

"I'm okay, Ans. What'chu doing?"

"I'm getting ready to make a gumbo since it finally decided to get cold."

She giggled as I played with the box in my pocket. I watched her put a pot of water on the stove, then I pulled her in my arms. "You know you're the best thing that has ever happened to me, right?"

She smiled, then put her hand to my face. "And you are one of the best things that have ever happened to me too."

My hand trembled as I grabbed hers and a concerned expression made its way to her face. "Jayden, you're trembling. What's wrong? Did I do something wrong?"

"Naw. You do everything right. The way you love me is just so right, Ans. No woman has ever made me feel the way you do. You have my heart and soul, baby. I love you so much."

She looked nervous, so I figured I better get this out the way. "I love you too, Jayden," she said hesitantly.

I continued to hold her hand as I went down on one knee. Her face had reddened significantly, and her breathing had become labored. "Ans, you are everything I want. Everything I need. Today is the day Remo gave me the green light to talk to you last year. We've come a long way since then, and I want to continue to progress in our relationship."

I pulled the box from my pocket and opened it to show her the beautiful chocolate solitaire diamond on a rose gold band encased in diamonds as well. "Ans, I want us to be forever. Please say you'll marry me."

"Jayden, oh my God," she said as she fanned herself with her hands.

"Ansley, I wanna be the man that you love forever. The man you choose to make love to. I wanna take care of you and the kids for life. But I can only do that if you let me." I wiped the tear from my cheek. "Tell me you gon' let me, Ansley."

"I'd be a fool not to let you. I'll marry you, Jayden."

The tears poured from her eyes as I slid the ring on her finger. I stood and lifted her in the air, spinning her around as she screamed. "Jayden!"

I laughed, then sat her on her feet and kissed her lips long and hard. Sliding my tongue in her mouth, Ansley moaned and held my face to hers. When she pulled away from me, she looked at her ring and screamed. "Jayden! This ring is gorgeous! I love it!"

"I'm glad. I can't wait to call you my wife."

"God, this is so unbelievable," she said, staring at her ring.

"It's so real though."

She went to the stove and turned the fire off. I stepped behind her and wrapped my arms around her waist, then kissed her neck. "I can't wait to show Alana."

I laughed loudly. "Don't be teasing my baby. I bought her a ring too."

"You did not!"

"I sure did. It's in the Range."

"Tell me it's not real."

"Naw, but my baby got some bling. Come on, let's go get them."

"School isn't out for another hour."

"Well, can we at least go get Lana?"

She rolled her eyes, and said, "Let's go."

When we got to Mr. and Mrs. Pierre's house and walked in the door, my baby girl ran to me. "Daddy!"

After I picked her up, she said, "Hey, Mommy!"

Ansley rolled her eyes. "Hey, girl. I got news for all of you!"

She was so excited, she was about to burst at the seams. Her parents stood from their seats, and Alana was frowning. All of them were waiting for what she was gonna say. "What news, Mommy?"

"We're gonna get married!" Ansley screamed, holding up her hand.

Her mama started screaming with her as Alana leaned over to look at the ring. She was still in my arms. "Mommy, let me see!"

Alana looked at it and frowned while Ansley smirked. She crossed her arms over her chest and looked back at me. "Daddy, you bought her a ring?"

I couldn't help but laugh. She referred to her mother like she was a random chick. Oh God, I had spoiled this little girl. I sat her on her feet, then got on my knee. "Did you think I would buy Ansley a ring and not buy you one?"

Her eyes brightened and she looked around at everyone smiling at her. I pulled the little ring from my pocket that mocked a diamond ring. "Alana, you are everything I want in a daughter. You love me with so much innocence and purity, that fills me with pride. Will you allow me to be your step-daddy?"

She looked at the ring, then back at me with those pretty hazel eyes. "No."

I frowned slightly but allowed her to continue. "You can be my daddy. I don't know what step-daddy means."

I smiled, then slid the ring on her finger as her eyes widened and her mouth opened. "Thank you, Daddy!"

She hugged me tightly, then kissed my cheek. I stood with her in my arms. Alana turned to Ansley, and with a big smile on her face, she asked, "So, when are we moving with Daddy?"

The End

AFTERWORD

From the Author

I truly hope you enjoyed reading this novel as much as I enjoyed writing it. There will be more drama-filled stories to read in the near future! There's also a great playlist on iTunes for this book under the same title. Please keep up with me on Facebook (@authormonicawalters), Instagram (@authormonicawalters), and Twitter (@monlwalters). You can also visit my Amazon author page at www.amazon.com/author/monica.walters to view my releases. For live discussions, giveaways, and inside information on upcoming releases, join my Facebook group, Monica's Romantic Sweet Spot at https://bit.ly/2P2lo6X.

T Key)

The Revelations of Ryan, Jr. (A Crossover Novel with All That Jazz by
T Key)

INDIA T. NORFLEET

B.LOVE PUBLICATIONS PRESENTS

THRILL MY
Soul

POETICALLY NASTY BY NATURE

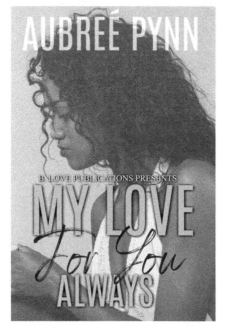

AUBREÉ PYNN

B.LOVE PUBLICATIONS PRESENTS

MY LOVE
For You
ALWAYS

B. LOVE PUBLICATIONS PRESENTS

Our
Secret
to Keep

an introduction

A. JONES

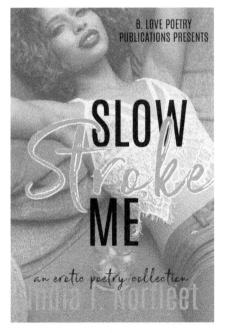

B. LOVE POETRY
PUBLICATIONS PRESENTS

SLOW
Stroke
ME

an erotic poetry collection

Jimma F. Norfleet

Aubreé Pynn

SAY HE'LL BE
My Valentine
The BLP "Say He" Series

SHENAÉ HAILEY

LOVE PUBLICATIONS
PRESENTS

WITH
ALL MY
heart

Visit bit.ly/readBLP to join our mailing list!

B. Love Publications - where Authors celebrate black men, black women, and black love.

To submit a manuscript for consideration, email your first three chapters to blovepublications@gmail.com with SUBMISSION as the subject.

Let's connect on social media!

Facebook - B. Love Publications

Twitter - @blovepub

Instagram - @blovepublications

CPSIA information can be obtained
at www.ICGtesting.com
Printed in the USA
LVHW111449011119
636084LV00003B/415/P